Mirabella and the Faded Phantom

Sharon Skinner

Brick Cave Media
brickcavebooks.com
2014

Brick Cave Media
brickcavebooks.com
2014

Also by Sharon Skinner

In Case You Didn't Hear Me the First Time
The Healer's Legacy
The Nelig Stones

The Matriarch's Devise*
Collars and Curses*

Also available from brickcavebooks.com

* Forthcoming

Dedication

To all the amazing teachers who gave me
encouragement and made me think.

Acknowledgements

I am once more indebted to my amazing editor, Anne
Lind, who read uncountable drafts and made
immeasurable contributions to the final manuscript.
Thanks to her, and a select group of awesome Beta
readers, Mirabella's story is much improved. Any
remaining mistakes or imperfections belong solely to
me.

A special thanks to my growing list of incredible fans.
Whenever I find myself struggling to grow a story into
the best it can be, I remind myself that there are
amazing readers who are looking forward to the next
book. Thank you for your support!

Mirabella and the Faded Phantom

Sharon Skinner

Veronica ~ Never give up the ghost! Sharon Skinner TCC 2014

Brick Cave Media
brickcavebooks.com
2014

CHAPTER ONE

Mirabella dropped her schoolbooks on top of a stack of unopened moving boxes and threw herself down onto her bed. She glared at the faded walls and unfamiliar furniture. A winter storm growled outside, rain rattling against the windows like handfuls of thrown gravel, and the old house creaked and groaned in the heavy wind. Mirabella sneezed, three quick explosions. She grabbed a tissue to wipe her already sore nose and let out a groan of her own. It wasn't bad enough they'd had to leave their apartment and move to this crummy town, but this creepy old house was practically made of dust. Horrible, nasty dust that attacked her nose like a bully goes after a little kid.

She wadded up the used tissue and tossed it into the trash can beside her bed. Her eyes began to prickle and she gave the room a sour look. No wonder her mother's Aunt had decided to sell the creaky old wreck and move to Florida. Unfortunately, no one else seemed to want it either. When the weather got cold, Great Aunt Clovinia headed south to move into her new condo. "My real estate agent says a lived-in home sells better than an empty one," she'd told Mirabella's mother. So they'd taken the bus to Robertsville and picked up the keys. The very next day, Mirabella's mother had gotten a nursing job working for Dr. Worth at the local medical clinic. Her mother called it serendipity. As far as Mirabella was concerned, there wasn't anything fortunate about her life these days.

She pushed her glasses up on her nose and reached for the book she was reading, but it wasn't on the nightstand where she'd left it. She leaned over the side of the bed, searching the floor. "I know I left it right beside the bed," she muttered.

A shushing sound whispered in Mirabella's ear and a cold gust of air slithered across the back of her neck. She jerked up and surveyed the room, catching her breath. Her book lay open on top of the tall dresser that leaned against the far wall.

"That's weird. How did it get there?" Mirabella narrowed her eyes at the errant book. "I know I left it right here on the nightstand."

She stalked over, picked up the book and riffled the pages. "What happened to my bookmark?"

Mirabella frowned. Her mom might be right about them having nowhere else to go, but Mirabella didn't have to like it. And she didn't have to like this drafty old house where nothing seemed to stay put.

"I hate this! I can hardly breathe in this place." Mirabella fell back onto the bed and watched as the socks her mother had piled in neat stacks tumbled down, the colors all mixing together. Not that it mattered. They'd just get all scrambled up in the drawer anyway. She blew her nose, again.

Back in their old apartment, her allergies almost never bothered her, except in the early spring. But ever since she'd set foot in this house, she'd been plagued with constant sneezing and sniffling, and she was so stuffed up she sounded like a honking goose whenever she talked.

She missed the snug little bedroom where her furniture had fit just right. This new room was so large she could have put three rooms the size of her old one into it. The ceiling rose high above her and the single overhead light cast a weak glow over everything.

Against one wall, a wrought-iron bedframe held a sagging mattress with ancient bedsprings that squeaked whenever Mirabella put any weight on it. Beside the bed, on a squat nightstand, her mother had arranged her radio clock and her purple desk lamp. A faded rug lay in the center of the room, and a bulging overstuffed chair took up most of the corner near the closet, a dark yawning space with a high shelf and a wooden dowel for hanging clothes.

All the furniture was sad and dreary looking, except for the vanity that sat against the wall opposite the bed. Mirabella had never seen a vanity before, but as soon as she'd laid eyes on this one, she'd decided she should always have one. It wasn't because the vanity was made to sit at and put on make-up. She would never smear that goop on her face. It was because the vanity was the most beautiful thing she'd ever seen. Made of pale polished wood the color of a golden palomino and carved with delicate roses that framed the oval mirror, the vanity seemed to sing to Mirabella every time she looked at it.

Mirabella sighed. She blew her nose again, took out her journal, opened it to a fresh page, and began to write:

Day 3 of the big move: Today I attended the Jeremiah Flesching Elementary School for the first time. I wish it was the last! They should rename it the Jerkemiah Flushing School!

Fifth grade homeroom is the land of the furry barn owl, better known as Mrs. Flizzer, English teacher. I think she can see the reflection of the students behind her in those thick glasses she wears. How else does she know when someone is doing something wrong when she's clearly facing the blackboard? She probably has a listening device hidden in that big, fuzzy sweater, too. Note: Watch for signs of espionage. Possible experiment: Hide glasses to see if she can still tell without looking when students aren't paying attention.

Second period: Math, land of the Troll. It's a good thing there are no billy goats in math class, or Mr. Pattison would probably eat them. Maybe he already has. Maybe that's why there aren't any. Possible experiment: Bring a goat to math class. Only, where would I get a goat? More research required.

Third period: Global Studies—

Achoo! Achoo, achoo! A series of sneezes exploded from Mirabella's nose.

She grabbed for another tissue, but a gust of cold air blew the thin paper just out of reach.

"There must be some huge cracks in this old house." She leaned forward and snatched at another tissue. A thin strip came away in her hand, but the rest of it stayed in the box. Mirabella groaned.

She pulled the box closer, peeled the rest of the torn paper out, and wiped her nose. She scrunched up the used tissue and threw it at the wastebasket. The wrinkly ball arced toward the basket, stopped in mid-air and flew back at her. It dropped onto the bed beside her, and she eyed it with suspicion before grabbing it. This time, she took careful aim and threw even harder, watching in amazement as the ball of paper soared back up and landed on the bed again.

Whoa! She jumped up to examine the trash can. *What could cause it to do that?* She began thinking about possible explanations for the ball's odd behavior. Obviously, an experiment was in order.

Mirabella picked up the wad of tissue and scrunched it into a tight mass. She threw the clump of paper at the trash can and watched it drop in and stay there. Mirabella made a face at the wastebasket.

She squished up another tissue, took aim, and threw. But just when the paper sphere should have dropped inside, it hurtled back and flew past her head. It hadn't been her imagination. But what would cause a tissue ball to defy gravity? Then she heard it. A low shushing sound, like the movement of that stiff taffeta party dress her mother had forced her to wear on her fifth birthday.

She stuck her finger in her mouth to wet it and held it up to feel for the draft that must be blowing through the middle of her bedroom. Only there didn't seem to be any air movement. And the sound had stopped. The room was as still as the inside of an undisturbed sarcophagus.

She slid off the bed and strode over to the wastebasket and stuck out her hand. No wind. She examined the basket, inside and out. Nothing. She wadded up another tissue, held it directly over the basket and let go. It plunged toward the opening, stopped, turned in mid air, and flew onto the bed.

A shiver streaked up her spine and she froze, heart thumping hard. *Calm down*, she told herself. *There has to be a scientific explanation.*

She balled up several tissues, checking their weight to make sure they were too heavy to be blown across the room even by a strong wind and dropped them. The tissue ball fell straight down, but instead of landing on the floor it shot back into the air, rose high overhead, and rebounded off the ceiling before plopping onto her dresser.

Her mouth fell open.

CHAPTER TWO

"Mira!" Mirabella's mother's shout ricocheted up the stairs. "Come down and eat."

Mirabella spun around. She backed out of the room and rocketed down the hallway, skidding to a halt on the landing. The door to her room stood open, pale light spilling out into the quiet hall. She chewed her thumbnail, thinking. There was no logical explanation for what had happened. Yet, she'd seen the tissue zipping around the room with her own eyes. She wanted to rush down the stairs and tell her mother all about it. Only, she'd never believe her. Mirabella wouldn't have believed it herself, if she hadn't seen it with her own eyes.

"Mira! Did you hear me?"

She jumped. Stupid house! She wrinkled up her nose and sneezed twice before clomping down the stairs, sniffling hard all the way into the kitchen.

"What a lovely sound," her mother said in her most

cheerful I-hope-you-know-I'm-joking voice. "I bet all the boys in school are in love with you already."

Mirabella snorted. "Boys are dumb. Who cares what they think?"

While her mother drained the pasta, Mirabella set the table and poured herself a glass of milk. Then she slid out a chair and sat down. The house had a separate dining room with a long table and eight chairs, but Mirabella's mother preferred to eat in the kitchen. She said it was cozier for two people, and it made cleaning up a lot easier, too, which was just fine with Mirabella.

Her mother set a bowl of salad onto the table and sat down across from her. Mirabella gripped the salad tongs and pinched three pieces of lettuce and a single cherry tomato onto her plate.

"You'll need four times that amount to make a serving."

Her mother's plate was piled high with salad. Ugh! "I'm not hungry," Mirabella said. "It's hard to eat when you can't breathe." She watched in horror as her mother scooped up a huge serving of salad and dropped it onto Mirabella's plate.

"You're not blue, yet."

Mirabella chewed on a mouthful of greens, wondering how long a person would have to go without breathing in order to turn blue. She had experimented a few times, holding her breath in front of the bathroom mirror, but she'd always found herself gasping for air before she saw even a tinge of blue.

"What did you learn in school, today?"

"Nothing." She forked another bite of salad into her mouth.

"You spent the entire day there and you didn't learn anything? With a mind as bright as yours, I find that difficult to believe."

"I did learn that there are sixteen classrooms in the four main buildings and three more in the portables." She pushed her salad around on her plate.

"Really? Anything else?"

Mirabella wanted to tell her mother about Mrs. Flizzer being a spy, but she wouldn't believe her. Not without proof. And getting proof would take some serious experimentation. She shook her head and sneezed.

"What about homework?"

"I already did it." Mirabella blew her nose into her napkin. "They're practically still in the dark ages in math and English is easy."

Her mother handed her a fresh napkin. "Perhaps I should speak with your teachers and see if they can't challenge you a little more."

"You're not serious, are you? The other kids will think I'm a total geek. And they already don't like me!"

"What do you mean they don't like you? You haven't been here long enough to get to know anyone."

"No one talks to me." Mirabella pushed a slice of mushroom to the side of her plate. "And they'll hate me even worse if they think I'm too smart."

"Do you really believe that?" Her mother lifted an eyebrow.

Mirabella raised her eyes to meet her mother's questioning look. "Yes."

"Well, if a few of them have a problem with intelligent girls, that's their loss. But I doubt every student in the entire school feels that way."

"All the ones in my classes do," Mirabella grumped.

"Fine. But if I find out you have too much time on your hands . . ." She waited for her words to sink in.

Mirabella tried to look innocent, but her mother's this-is-serious-business gaze seemed to pierce right through her skin and into her bones.

"That means no pranks."

"They're not pranks. They're—"

"Experiments. Right." It was her I'm-indulging-you voice. "No experiments, then."

"But Mom!"

"No experiments. And no buts, or you'll find yourself not only doing extra schoolwork, but grounded till you're twenty-one."

And no saying anything about what just happened in my room, Mirabella thought, wiping her nose.

"I'm sorry the dust is irritating your allergies, but you needn't be so dramatic. Living here will allow us to put aside some money so we can get a nice place of our own." She gave Mirabella her everything-is-going-to-work-out-fine-just-wait-and-see look. "And need I remind you that if your Great Aunt Clovinia hadn't offered us this house temporarily, we'd have nowhere to live?"

Why did mothers have to act like they were right about everything?

It wasn't fair that the clinic in the city where they used to live had closed and her mother had lost her job. It wasn't fair that they'd had to move to this worn-out house in this dumpy little town. Most of all, it wasn't fair that she hadn't been allowed to see her father, or say good-bye. A chill flowed over her and she caught an especially huge sneeze in her napkin.

"I can't breathe," Mirabella grumbled.

"If you couldn't actually breathe, you wouldn't be able to complain about it, Mira," her mother said. "You'll feel better once we get the house cleaned up."

"I won't feel better. I hate this town. I hate the school. And I hate this stinky, dirty house!" Mirabella stared at the wall, thinking that if her eyes were lasers, she could burn a hole all the way through the horrible, creaky house.

Mirabella's mother put on her I'm-counting-to-ten-so-I-can-discuss-this-with-you-calmly face. "Mira, I know it isn't easy to pull up roots and move without warning the way we did. But we'd have been out on the street with nowhere to go rather than snug in this house, if not for Aunt Clovinia. I'm sure you'll grow to like it here." She gazed around the narrow kitchen. "I know I always have."

Mirabella snorted, but a stern look from her mother turned the snort into another sneeze.

"The least you can do is to give it a chance." Her mother frowned at her. "If not for all the pranks you pulled, the apartment manager might not have been so quick to take action when we missed the rent payment."

"I told you, those weren't pranks. They were psychological experiments." Mirabella dabbed at her sore nose.

"Grape jelly in the mailboxes? What kind of psychological experiment is that?"

Mirabella frowned. It hadn't been Mirabella who had put the jelly in the mailboxes. Why wouldn't her mother believe her? She suspected the kids from upstairs. It certainly wasn't any kind of psychological experiment she would have tried. It just turned everyone's mail purple. And sticky.

Especially sticky.

She'd tried to tell her mother at the time that she'd never do anything so pointless. But, of course, her mom hadn't listened. No one else had believed her either. They'd all just blamed her. Mirabella's fist clamped hard around her fork. Her father would have believed her, but of course he hadn't been there.

She shoved away the painful missing that tried to swallow her and turned her laser beam eyes on her mother. It had taken days to clean the gooey mess out of all the boxes in the apartment's tiny lobby. "But that wasn't—"

"I don't know what you were thinking." Her mother cut her

off, in her I-don't-want-to-hear-you-telling-lies-so-I-suggest-you-rethink-what-you're-saying voice.

Mirabella would have liked to convince her mother that the jelly wasn't her, but she decided to let it go, since there were several other things she'd rather her mother didn't bring up. Like the fake baseball in the windshield she'd stuck on the pastor's car that caused his face to turn the brightest shade of red she'd ever seen, and everyone else to suffer through an extra long sermon that Sunday.

"And you nearly frightened Mrs. MacNeally to death when you put that recording in the laundry room and made it sound like someone was stuck in the dryer."

Mirabella sniffed. "How else could I find out if she would have helped if I'd been trapped in there?"

"In the first place, even if you were silly enough to have squeezed yourself into that old dryer, the door latch was so loose it barely kept the clothes from falling out when they were drying. So, you would have been able to free yourself." Her mother shook her head. "And in the second place, you could have just asked her what she would do if something like that were to happen."

Mirabella jabbed her fork into a tomato, watching in satisfaction as the juice squirted onto the table. "People can't tell you what they'd do when faced with a life or death situation. They don't know how they'll react until the situation happens."

"Who told you that?" Her mother's voice was sharp.

It was her father she'd heard it from, but she didn't want her mother to know that. "I must have read it somewhere." It was possible, so not really a lie, right?

"Mira, you can't believe everything you read. And even if it is true, that's no reason to go scaring the life out of people."

Mirabella stared at her plate. "I said I was sorry."

"I know, Mira, but sometimes being sorry after the fact doesn't fix things." She pushed a lock of curls out of Mirabella's eyes. "It will get better. I promise. The first day at a new school is always the hardest." Her mother tilted her head to the side and her face softened. "After the dishes are done, we can get out the game box, if you want."

Games? Mirabella thought. We haven't played games since Dad— Her food stuck in her throat.

It wasn't fair! First her father and mother had split up. They said it was supposed to be a trial separation, but Mirabella could tell they were just saying that so she wouldn't be upset. Then, just when she'd gotten used to only seeing her father every other weekend, everything had changed.

Forever.

The laser beams were suddenly back in her eyes, but now they seemed to be trapped inside. She kept the tears from falling, but her plate became a bleary spot of running colors. She stabbed at her food, poking it with her fork until her mother gave her the evil eye.

She started to say it. To tell her mother how much she missed him. But her mother would only change the subject again, the way she always did when Mirabella brought up her father. And she had no one else to talk to. She never would, now. She took a gulp of milk to help her swallow her food. There was no point in thinking about it. He was gone and nothing in the world could change that.

CHAPTER THREE

"Time's up," Mrs. Flizzer said. "Trade papers with the person next to you and we'll correct them."

Kids groaned as they passed their papers to their classmates. Mirabella held her paper out to the girl in the next row. The girl's dark eyes narrowed to glittery slits, and her lips turned down in a lopsided frown as she took the paper between thumb and forefinger and dropped it onto her desk. She rolled her eyes as she handed over her own paper. Suddenly, the girl yanked out a red marker and pulled off the cap with a flourish. She grinned with glee, the pen held above the paper in obvious anticipation.

The red marker smelled like cherries soaked in chemicals. Mirabella's nose twitched. Gross! She pinched her nose to stop herself from sneezing all over her desk. The girl with the smelly marker sneered at her.

Mirabella shot a look around the room. The girl she had traded papers with looked older than most of the kids in the class. More like a sixth-grader. She read the name in the upper right hand corner of the paper: Stacey Hollis. Big loopy letters with swirling curls at the end of each word filled the page, every small i dotted with a circle that hovered above the letter like a halo. Mirabella glanced at the girl's mean-looking grin. Stacey Hollis sure didn't look like an angel.

She read through the list of spelling words on the paper in front of her. Four out of the twelve words were misspelled. She raised her pencil to check off the words and stopped.

Stacey glared at her, lips curled in menace.

Mirabella put down her pencil and waited as the teacher called on first one person, then another, to spell the words aloud. She dutifully checked off the misspelled words only after the teacher confirmed them as wrong. When she traded Stacey's paper for her own, she saw that six of the twelve words on her paper had huge red check marks next to them.

"These are spelled right," she told the girl.

"Really?"

"Yes."

"Sorry. The handwriting was so bad, I couldn't tell." Stacey grabbed the paper back and crossed off the check marks, turning them into giant red chemical-cherry smelling blobs. Then she tossed the page back onto Mirabella's desk.

Mrs. Flizzer stopped writing the new set of vocabulary words on the board and turned to face them. "Is there something you'd like to share with the class?"

"Sorry, Mrs. Flizzer," Stacey said, her face full of innocence. "I was just helping the new girl with her penmanship."

Mrs. Flizzer raised an eyebrow, but Mirabella said nothing. Stacey smiled sweetly until Mrs. Flizzer went back to writing on the board. Then she made a bug-eyed face at Mirabella.

When the buzzer signaled the end of class, Stacey got up

from her desk, flicked her long hair over her shoulders, and kicked over Mirabella's messenger bag, sending her books and papers sliding across the floor. Then she sauntered out of the classroom without a word. Mirabella's hands shook as she shoveled her books back into her bag before hurrying to her next class.

In the hallway, kids rushed past her on their way to their classes. Mirabella stared toward the exit. For the first time in her life, she wanted to leave school in the middle of the day. Her feet dragged her down the hall toward the double doors that led to freedom. But she couldn't skip school. Her father had never missed a day of work, and she'd hardly missed a day of school since kindergarten.

She turned around and bumped into a thin boy with spiky black hair, who mumbled a quick, "sorry," and kept going. The rest of the hall was empty now, and Mirabella had to run to get to class before the second buzzer.

CHAPTER FOUR

Another storm battered the house. With each blast of thunder, the lights flickered and threatened to go out. Mirabella sat on her bed, documenting her day. Frigid air laced itself around her, sliding frozen fingers beneath the comforter draped over her shoulders.

A satiny hiss erupted near her ear. Startled, Mirabella glanced around the room.

Nothing out of place.

It must have been the rain. A crack of thunder rattled her bedroom window and she flinched. She pulled the comforter tighter and bent over her journal, but as the pen connected with the page the sound came again.

Louder. And nearer.

This time there was no clap of thunder. Even the wind seemed to have died down and the clatter of rain against the glass had changed to a soft patter like fingers tapping against a thick quilt. Mirabella turned her head in the direction of the hissing and squinted.

Again, nothing.

She shrugged and turned back to her writing, but the shushing sound spouted again, right in her ear, and what felt like icy tendrils trailed along her face and neck. Her arm snapped up, and she swished it through the air in front of her. Something hissed again and a wet chill wrapped around her wrist and crawled toward her shoulder.

Mirabella spun around and leaped off the bed, rubbing her arm and staring at the place where she'd felt the iciness. A blurry spot swam in the air. She took off her glasses, cleaned them on her shirt, then put them back on. The blur had shifted, but was still visible.

Her hands shook as she rechecked her glasses. Clean.

One step at a time, Mirabella crept toward the place where the wall turned from a distinct shade of lavender to a fuzzy gray. Just a little closer. The spot wavered. She extended her arm toward the wall.

The blur slid away from her fingertips.

She snapped her hand away, backing across the room in a rush. The spot now hovered an arm's length to the left of where it had been.

Mirabella twisted her mouth sideways, thinking. Was this some kind of psychological experiment? Sure, her mother said she had to go to the store for milk, but that could have been the set-up. Her mother could easily be playing a trick to show her what it felt like to be the scientific subject.

"Mom?" she called.

No answer. But that didn't mean her mother wasn't in the house.

She stuck her head out into the hall. "Okay, Mom. I get it." The house was quiet. Too quiet. Aside from the splatter of rain on the roof, there wasn't a creak or a groan.

Ka-pow! A clap of thunder exploded right over the house and Mirabella let out a squeal.

The hissing sound came again, this time sounding like a steam locomotive.

Mirabella whipped around and glimpsed the outline of a person sitting on the edge of her bed. But as she stared, the image faded to a blur.

She took off her glasses and rubbed her eyes. The blurriness remained there, hanging near the edge of her bed like a piece of nearly invisible gauze. It floated above the mattress, folded over the edge and puddled on the floor.

She stared at the fuzzy place on the floor. The haziness thickened there, like it really was a puddle of something. She continued to stare at the spot, letting her eyes get lazy, the way she had to in order to see those special puzzles, the ones that appeared to be a mix of colors and swirls until her eyes relaxed and she saw a three-dimensional image. Slowly, the puddle became the vague outline of a pair of feet.

Mirabella didn't move. She didn't breathe. She didn't think. Was the room shaking? No. It was her. All of her. Shivering. From toes to head. But not from cold. Her unsteady gaze climbed from the feet and up the—legs? No. More like the lumpy outline of legs, then up to where shoulders and a head should be. The shadowy shape grew more defined, but the head remained a roundish lump.

"What—" Mirabella began.

The figure bobbed up off the bed. "Oooh!" The word rasped out in a chafing whisper like the sound of a panting dog.

"Oh!" Mirabella echoed. She wanted to run, but her legs wobbled and her feet ignored the signals from her brain.

"You can see me?" the figure asked.

A tight feeling crawled around inside Mirabella's mouth, strangling her voice. She nodded.

"Oh my!" the figure said. "That's new!"

"It is?" Mirabella asked, curiosity winning out over fear.

"Yes. At least, as far as I can recall." The shape wavered, fluttering like a flag in a soft breeze.

If this is some sort of trick, Mirabella thought now that her heart had quit thudding triple-time, I don't want to act scared, or worse, stupid. She glanced around the room. Her mother might be hiding somewhere, watching. But where? The closet door gaped open, just as she had left it, and moving boxes still filled the space under the bed. There wasn't anywhere else in the room where a person could hide. The dresser hunched against the wall, and the vanity with its long legs and curved edges was too low and narrow for anyone to hide behind without being seen.

Mirabella glanced at the window. Nothing. Only the bruised darkness of the overcast sky. She started to search the ceiling for holes where spy cameras might lurk, but her attention was drawn back to the filmy figure. It seemed to be pulsing. Not much. Just a soft change of light that came and went in cadence, like the rhythm of a heartbeat.

She wondered what she should say. It had to be something clever, so her mom would know she wasn't fooled. "Is there some reason I shouldn't be able to see you?" she asked.

"No. Or maybe, yes? I'm not actually certain." The figure pulsed faster, brighter.

"Then why do you think it is that I can?" Mirabella peeked over her shoulder at the dimly lit hall. Still no Mom. No one at all.

No one, that is, except the apparition in her room.

"I don't know." Flash. Flash. Flash.

"You don't seem to know much, do you?" Mirabella twisted her fingers together, thinking she should be able to unravel this puzzle. After all, she'd performed enough experiments of her own to have a good idea what it took to make one work. But she had no idea how this one was being done.

The figure flickered like a Halloween party strobe light. Then it went out.

Mirabella rushed to the bed and swept her arms through the air. There was nothing there. No visible trace of what she had seen. Only a chill in the air and a cold spot on the bed where the figure had been sitting remained, along with the faint, sweet odor of flowers.

CHAPTER FIVE

"Hello?" Mirabella called out. But there was no answer. No sound at all except the splatter of rain against the dark window.

Ripping back the bedding, she swiped her hands across the mattress. Nothing. She yanked open one dresser drawer after the other, tossing the clothes aside and running her hands over the bottoms of the drawers. A rapid search of the rest of the room revealed nothing unusual. No cameras, no projectors, no electronics.

She ran from her bedroom and raced down the hall, peering into each room she passed, looking for her mother, or some sign of video equipment, anything that might be used to make a glowing figure seem to appear and disappear.

She finished checking the upstairs and headed for the ground floor. As she entered the kitchen, the door swung open squeaking on its hinges. A streak of lightning silhouetted the dark figure that bulked in the doorway.

With a yelp, Mirabella skidded to a stop. She spun around

and sped into the dining room, looking for a place to hide.

The kitchen door swung shut with a bang. The figure sloshed into the room and turned on the light. "Mirabella! Quit fooling around and come help me with these groceries."

"Mom?" Was that shrill sound her voice? It sounded more like a dog's squeak toy.

"Who did you think it was? The ghost of Christmas past?" Her mother hung her raincoat on the hook by the door and kicked off her soggy boots. "What's gotten into you?" She gave Mirabella her why-are-you-behaving-this-way look.

Mirabella crept into the kitchen and scanned the room. "Nothing. You scared me, that's all." She stood at the kitchen table and peered into the grocery bags.

Her mother stepped into her fuzzy slippers and placed her boots on the doormat to dry. "Sorry. I guess I forgot how eerie this house can be when you're all alone. Your Grandmother Marita even refused to sleep here."

"Why?" Mirabella had been very young when Grandmother Marita had died, but she remembered how much fun she'd been. And how she'd always insisted that Mirabella call her G'ma, only she pronounced it "Geemaw."

G'ma Marita had lived in a squat little house set back in the woods where she let the trees and bushes grow right up to the house. She had also insisted that Mirabella keep a watch out for sprites and other strange creatures lurking in the woods. Watching for the tree sprites had been one of Mirabella's favorite games until she discovered that her parents and the other adults shook their heads every time the old woman talked about it. Somehow, Mirabella understood that none of the grownups, except for G'ma Marita, believed in the sprites.

Her mother began to pull groceries out of the bags, sorting them onto the table. "She thought the place was haunted. Isn't that silly?"

"Yeah. Silly." Mirabella's hand shook as she put the jug of milk into the refrigerator. "What made her think that?"

"Oh, the usual. Drafts. Cold spots. She actually claimed that something moved her things around. After a while, she refused to stay here. She'd take a room at Farmingale's Bed & Breakfast when she came to visit. I pointed it out when we drove into town. Remember?"

"Did Aunt Clovinia think the house was—you know—haunted?"

"I don't think so. At least, she never said anything about it to me. Oh, leave those out," she pointed to the box of crackers. "We're having soup for dinner. Nothing like hot soup to warm you up from the inside on a cold day." She rubbed her arms. "Grandmother Marita was right about one thing."

Mirabella froze, her hand on a jar of dill pickles. "What?"

"This house is full of chills and drafts."

CHAPTER SIX

The school day dragged on like a holiday church sermon. Mirabella squirmed, tilting her head to see the clock without being obvious. No point in giving the teachers a reason to single her out. Again. Her face was probably still red from this morning when Mr. Pattison held up her homework as an example of "splendid work tidily presented." He'd gone on and on about it. Bad enough to be new, but now everyone knew she was smart. And a neat freak, too. So much for making any friends. Ever.

Not that she needed any of them! Having a friend would just get in the way of her new experiments. She was sure to prove her mother had been behind the things that had happened in the house. Then, she'd be able to do her own experiments again. Her mom couldn't expect to have it both ways. Anyway, a friend would expect her to hang out and spend time talking on the phone, maybe even go to the movies or come to a birthday party.

She stuck her chin on her fist and stared at her Science book, but she couldn't focus. The words all looked the same. Blah, blah, blah.

Her mother had said that G'ma Marita thought the house was haunted. But then, G'ma had thought pixies lived in her garden. Even believed they spoke to her. Besides, there were no such things as ghosts. Right?

She fiddled with her pencil, tapping the eraser end against the pages of her book. *Tap, tap, tap.* If only she had a camera. Better yet, a video camera. *Tap, tap.* Then she could record the phenomenon. *Tap, tap, tap.* She could study the video and then she'd know if someone was hoaxing her or not. *Tap, tap, tap.*

A hand reached out and covered her pencil, holding it still. Mirabella looked up into the unhappy face of Mr. Haley, the Science teacher. His dark stare told her she was in trouble.

"Mizz Polidoro," he said with his heavy southern drawl. "Ah am surprised at you. Is there some reason you have for not respondin' to mah question?"

Question? Had she been so distracted she hadn't heard the teacher call on her?

"I was reading?" She hadn't intended it to sound like a question, but maybe he hadn't noticed.

Unfortunately, the girl sitting behind her had and let out a soft giggle. Mr. Haley turned his eyes on the girl, but it was too late. The whole class burst into laughter. By the time Mr. Haley got them quiet, the bell had rung.

Mirabella stuffed her books into her messenger bag and slunk out of the room before Mr. Haley could stop her. If she was lucky, he would forget all about it by Monday. And so would the rest of the class.

CHAPTER SEVEN

The town library smelled of books. New books, old books, picture books, atlases. The one good thing about Robertsville was the old main library that stood near city hall. Pillars fronted either side of the door, and a life-size marble statue of the town's founder, a book in one hand and an oil lantern in the other, guarded the lobby of the building. Mirabella gazed around the room at the rows of tall bookshelves filled to overflowing and took a deep breath. The familiar scent comforted her. She'd always been an avid reader, but after her father died, books had become her best friends. Actually, her only friends.

The fat encyclopedia on the table in front of her was full of scientific information. Open to a section on holograms, the book's pages arched outward. She traced her finger along the smooth page, moving it under each word of the sentence as she read it again.

"There is no current technology outside of a laboratory to

project a real life-sized, moving, talking hologram that permits a person to walk all the way around and view it from all sides."

Mirabella closed the book. If the figure appeared again, all she had to do was walk all the way around it. Easy. But what if it wasn't a hologram? She shook her head. It had to be. There wasn't anything else it could be. And when she caught her mother experimenting on her, she would have the perfect excuse to begin her own experiments again.

Happily, she gathered up her papers and stuffed them into her book bag. A sticky note stuck to the back of her math assignment grabbed her attention. Ghosts and Haunted Houses 133.1 R393Z 1947. She had found the book in the library's online catalog, but she hadn't pulled it off the shelf. What was the point? What she'd seen in her room had to be a hologram. Right? She shoved the paper in with her books and shrugged the bag onto her shoulder, but the numbers kept nagging her. 133.1 R393Z 1947. 133.1 R393Z 1947.

What could it hurt? It would at least be interesting to read. "Better than reading *Taming the Forest* again," she muttered.

"Excuse me," a high voice whispered right behind her.

Mirabella spun around and faced the owner of the voice. She recognized the girl from school. She had large blue eyes and a long nose. Her straight brown hair, streaked with blonde, hung down to the middle of her back. Mirabella stared.

"Hi," the girl said. "Did I hear you say you've already read *Taming the Forest*?"

"Um, yeah." Mirabella puffed at her bangs, trying to blow her dark curls out of her eyes. She wished her hair was straight like this girl's, then maybe it would be easier to comb. She might even be able to brush it.

"Wow! That's great." People looked up from their reading and someone shushed them. The girl covered her mouth, glanced around and grimaced. Then she lowered her voice to a whisper. "Tell me about it."

Mirabella shrugged. "I thought it was okay. The factual details seemed to be accurate."

"No. I mean, tell me what it's about. We have a book report due on it and I haven't actually read it. Yet."

Mirabella tilted her head to one side and squinted at the girl.

"Sorry. My name's Erin. Hi." The girl grinned and bent her elbow, arm tight against her side, and held up her hand waving it back and forth in short bursts.

She must think that's really cute, Mirabella thought. She raised her hand, then let it drop. "Hi."

"You're new here, aren't you?"

"Yes."

"What's your name?"

"Mirabella."

"That's a really different name."

"I guess so," Mirabella said. She decided not to tell Erin that her father had named her, or that Mirabella meant fantastic in Italian. He'd also said her black curly hair had come from his Italian roots, and that she should be proud of it. But Mirabella still wished she could have any other kind of hair than what she'd been stuck with.

"So, what's the book about?"

Mirabella glanced down at the heavy volume lying on the table. "It's an encyclopedia."

"Not that book. *Taming the Forest*." Erin tilted her head sideways and stared at Mirabella quizzically. "It's all about surviving in the wilderness and eating berries and stuff, right?"

"Right."

"What else? Does anybody die or anything big happen?"

"Why don't you read it and find out?"

29

Erin shrugged. "It would be a whole lot easier if you just told me about it. Besides, if any animals die, I'll hate it."

Mirabella mashed her lips together for a moment, considering. "That wouldn't really be right," she said. "I mean, you're supposed to read it yourself."

"I know that." Erin swept her long hair back over her shoulder with one hand. "It's just that I haven't had time, you know, and the report's due, and I thought if you could tell me about it, I could write the report now and read the book later."

"If you haven't already read the book, why should I believe you'll read it after you've done the report?" Mirabella tried not to grimace as she heard her mother's words coming out of her own mouth.

Erin shrugged, all innocence. "Because I said I would."

Mirabella frowned. She didn't know this girl. Why should she do anything for her? Then again, if she helped Erin with her report, maybe she'd have a friend, or at least someone to talk to. She opened her mouth, but snapped it shut again when she saw Stacey Hollis stalking toward them.

"Hey, Erin!" Stacey called.

Erin grinned and gave Stacey her cutesy wave. "Hi Stace."

"What's up?" Stacey directed her gaze at Erin, but stuck her chin in Mirabella's direction.

"This is Marberella," Erin said.

"It's Mirabella," Mirabella corrected her.

Erin shrugged her shoulders. "She was just telling me about a book."

"What book is that?" Stacey asked.

"*Taming the Forest.* You know, the one we have to read for Mrs. Flizzer's class."

Stacey smirked. "Yeah. I know. It's lame. Why would you ask Marbles about it?"

Mirabella cringed inside. There it was, the dreaded

nickname. And this one was even worse than the old one. She'd hated Mirror Ball, but Marbles! She could already hear the rhymes the other kids would come up with and the cracks they'd make. It wouldn't be long before someone would call her Lost Yer Marbles or Loose Marbles.

"She said she read it already and I figured she could tell me what it's about," Erin said.

"I read it last year when my brother was in Mrs. Flizzer's class. I'll tell you all about it on the way home. Come on." Stacey swung around, smacking Mirabella with her backpack, then sashayed off without apologizing.

"Okay," Erin hitched her book bag up on her shoulder. "Bye, Marbles." She giggled and waved as she followed Stacey out the door.

Mirabella stared after them for a moment before carrying the encyclopedia over and plunking it down onto the shelving cart. "I hate this place," she muttered.

CHAPTER EIGHT

Mirabella sat on her bed, waiting for the figure to reappear. She tried to read, but the words jumped around on the page and she had trouble making sense of them. As soon as her mother had left the house, she'd headed upstairs. That had been over twenty minutes ago. It seemed a safe bet that the trick would only be effective if Mirabella was alone in the house. At least, that's the way she would have planned this type of experiment.

She shut the book and stared into the darkness outside her window. Maybe it was the clear weather that was wrong. Maybe the storm was one of the experimental parameters. Part of the set-up. It made sense. What could be spookier than being alone in a creaky old house on a dark and stormy night? Although, this old house was eerie even without the thunder and lightning and the window-rattling rain and wind.

Seconds stretched out and the numbers on the digital clock on the bedside table refused to change.

"Come on," she grumbled, swinging her legs over the side

of the bed. The room stood silent and empty of holograms. She flopped back, her head sinking into the pillow while she stared up at the ceiling. Maybe this time her mother really had just gone to the store.

Sighing, she rolled off the bed and reached under the mattress for her journal, but it wasn't there. She slid her hand further in. Nothing. Kneeling on the floor, she pushed up the edge of the mattress and peered into the space between the mattress and box springs. No journal.

Her chest pounded. It was gone! Her mother would never take it, would she? Mirabella tore the blankets and sheets off the bed. Pushed the mattress aside. Still nothing.

"No!" she shouted. "That's not fair."

"What's not fair?"

"Taking my . . . " Mirabella spun around. "Who said that?"

"I did," came a whispery response.

Mirabella took a step backward, tripped and tumbled onto the pile of bedding heaped on the floor.

Sibilant laughter burst from the corner of the room. The ghostly form took shape, and the flowery smell filled the room.

Mirabella scrambled to her feet. From where she stood, the hazy figure looked three-dimensional. She sidestepped to the right. The form still appeared fully rounded. She scooted back the left. There was no flattening of the image. But she couldn't be certain without walking all the way around it, and she couldn't do that with it standing in the corner. *Think, Mirabella, think*. Could holograms move from place to place? She couldn't remember.

"What are you doing?" the figure asked.

Can't let on, Mirabella thought. If she gave away her plan too soon, her mother might turn off the machine she was using to cast the figure into the room. "Oh, I'm just practicing my sideways running for PE," she said with a grimace and slid across the room again.

"PE?"

"Yep. Physical Education. You know, 'kids need exercise,'" Mirabella quoted her old PE teacher between breaths.

"Do you do those jumping things, too?"

"Jumping things?" Mirabella scooted back across the room.

"Yes." The figure floated out to the middle of the room. It raised its arms over its head and brought them down to its sides, rising and falling with the movement.

Mirabella stopped running from side to side and watched, fascinated by the bobbing figure. "Jumping Jacks," she said. "It looks like you're doing Jumping Jacks." She tilted her head to one side and watched the floor beneath the apparition. "Only you're doing them without touching the ground."

The figure stopped bobbing. "The children seemed to enjoy them."

Mirabella suddenly remembered what she needed to do. She moved around the shape, making a full circuit. The apparition remained three-dimensional from every angle.

With a gasp, Mirabella backed away.

"Are you doing more PE exercises?" The figure floated toward her. "I don't remember one quite like that. But then, there is so much I don't remember." It wavered, becoming nearly transparent.

The voice trembled with sorrow and Mirabella felt a sob pushing its way out of her chest. She reached for a tissue to wipe at her moist eyes, then stopped and stared as the figure faded completely. She spun around, searching the room for some sign of what she'd seen, but there was nothing.

What was that thing? Obviously not a hologram. But what else could it be? Could the house actually be haunted like G'ma said? Or was Mirabella seeing things? Could her mind be playing tricks on her?

Her legs felt wobbly. One careful step at a time, she crossed the room to her bed.

There on the nightstand lay her journal, open to the last entry.

Yesterday's date headed the page and the green ink doodles she had drawn down the left margin still looked like drooping alien flowers. She reread the words she had written about school. Had it been here the whole time? Had she somehow left it out? But she was certain she'd placed it under the corner of her mattress like always.

Who could have moved it? Her mother had promised years ago that she would never read Mirabella's personal journal. So, why was it lying out now?

"Hello?" she called. Her voice echoed back at her from the faded walls.

She snatched up the journal. A small sheet of paper fell from the pages and floated to the floor. She picked it up and stared at the picture of her father, and the caption beneath it.

In Loving Memory . . .

She shoved the paper back into the journal, slammed it shut, and stuffed it under the mattress.

CHAPTER NINE

Mirabella slunk down in her desk, wondering if she'd ever learn to keep her big mouth shut. But no, she just had to correct the teacher.

And be right.

Mr. Klutter had been good-natured about it. Too good-natured. In fact, she wished he'd just let it drop. But he was going on and on about having the courage to speak up, even in the face of authority. He'd been talking about it for almost the whole class now and the other students took turns glaring at Mirabella, like it was her fault.

Okay, so it was her fault, in a way. But it wasn't like she knew he would turn it into a huge long lecture. He made it seem like she'd done something great, like Rosa Parks when she refused to sit in the back of the bus, or Susan B. Anthony, who helped get the law changed so women could vote. When really all Mirabella had done was correct his timeline for the development of the United States space program. And she'd only known it was wrong because her dad had taught her all about the space race.

"You should all follow the example of your new classmate. Always question authority. Always!" Mr. Klutter pounded his fist on the desk and a tall stack of papers toppled over in slow motion. Frozen in place, Mr. Klutter watched the papers slide across the desk, slip over the edge and flutter to the floor. He flicked his eyes toward the class and his mouth curved up at the corners. "Don't try this at home," he said, then took a running start and landed with each foot on a different sheet of paper. He skated across the floor for a second before lurching to a stop and toppling forward. He tried to catch his balance, arms spinning like windmills, before splat-landing on his hands and knees.

Two boys on the left side of the room started to laugh and soon the whole room was roaring. With a small grimace, Mr. Klutter, got up, brushed the dust off his pants, and retrieved the scattered papers, turning them one way and another to put them back in order.

Embarrassed now more for Mr. Klutter than for herself, Mirabella slid further down in her seat. She focused on the open Global Studies book on her desk, her nose shoved so close to the text she couldn't actually make out the words.

When the buzzer sounded the end of class, she kept her head down and waited for the room to empty. Books slammed and backpacks zipped. Footsteps pounded past her and receded down the hall until the only sounds were the shushing of the eraser on the board and Mr. Klutter muttering to himself about authority and protesting and non-acceptance.

Silently, she closed her book and slid it into her school bag, then tiptoed toward the door. But just as she reached the hallway, someone tapped her on the arm.

With a start, Mirabella spun around, her bag held in front of her like a shield.

"Due diligence, young lady, but let's not act paranoid or they'll start to think we're conspiracy nuts," Mr. Klutter said with a wink. "It's one thing to be smart, but you don't want to give people the idea you're unstable because of it."

Mirabella stared at him. Unstable? Like crazy? Is that what she was? She'd always thought she was logical like her dad. He'd always made it seem like science could explain everything. But now she was seeing ghosts.

Did Mr. Klutter know? Was that why he said what he did? Was he warning her not to say anything? Or was he talking about himself and his strange behavior in front of the class? Skating on papers was something a kid might do, not a grown up. On the other hand, if he hadn't fallen, it would have been kind of cool.

"You dropped your pen." He held out her favorite purple roller ball.

"Oh." Mirabella took the pen and tucked it into the side pocket of her bag. "Thank you." She started to leave, but stopped. "I'm sorry I corrected you, Mr. Klutter."

"Nonsense," he said. "Don't apologize. You were right. You keep on correcting me when I'm wrong. I'm the one who should apologize for giving out bad information. And I should also thank you."

"For what?"

"For giving me an opportunity to speak out about something so important. It isn't every day a teacher is given a chance to use a real life example in the classroom. Not without having to set up for it in advance anyway." He gave her a lopsided grin.

The warning buzzer buzzed and kids brushed past them into the classroom. Mirabella dashed down the hall to Science class. Had she stepped right into a set-up? Had Mr. Klutter really made a mistake, or had he written the wrong information on the board on purpose, hoping someone would correct him? Either way, the other kids would like her even less now. Not only had she shown off how smart she was, she'd also caused a teacher to give a really boring speech about standing up to people when you know you're right.

She reached her next class, out of breath, and out of time. The final buzzer sounded just as she opened the door.

Mr. Haley handed her a stack of papers as she slid into her seat. "As the last person into the room," he said, "You may have the honor of handing out today's quiz."

She handed out the papers, pretending not to hear the buzzing complaints of her classmates blaming her for having to take a quiz.

CHAPTER TEN

Standing in the hall outside her bedroom, Mirabella stared in fascination, watching the ghost sway back and forth. The filmy figure spun across the floor, twirling in time to the song that rose up from the stereo system in the living room. The music was what her mother called "big band," and it was turned up super loud so her mom could hear it over the growl and whoosh of their ancient vacuum cleaner.

The ghost whirled around the room in a cloud of swirling vapor.

"Hi." Mirabella stepped into the room.

The filmy mist slowed to a stop. "Oh, hello, again."

"You like this kind of music?"

The ghostly fog coalesced into its familiar shapeless form. "Yes. I . . . seem to." It glided closer to the open bedroom door. "It reminds me of something . . . or someone . . . nice."

The figure was more defined than it had been before, and Mirabella thought she could make out a bow-shaped mouth and turned-up nose. But as she stared, the ghost's features became hazy and indistinct once more.

"I've been reading about you," Mirabella said.

"About me?" The figure leaned toward her.

"Well, not you exactly, but about, you know, what you are."

The figure grew hazier. "What do you mean?"

"Um, well, I found this book on spirits and haunted houses." Mirabella said.

"Spirits?" The ghost wavered and sank toward the floor.

"Yes. It says that there's a reason that spirits stay grounded, that means attached, to a single place. Like, you know, a house. Like this one."

"Do you mean—" The figure trembled, its edges fluttering like lace-edged curtains in a soft breeze. "You're talking about me?"

"Well, more about ghosts in general. But it seems to include you, too."

"Y—You mean I'm a—a ghost?"

Mirabella hesitated. Didn't it know? "I'm not sure how else to explain why you're here. Or why you appear and disappear the way you do."

"But, that can't be!" The phantom backed away from Mirabella. "You must be mistaken. I'm sure I don't believe in ghosts. At least, I don't think I do. Besides, where are the rattling chains?" It held out its arms to show Mirabella they were free of shackles. "And why aren't you frightened of me?"

"I—I'm sorry." Mirabella held up the book on haunted houses. "But from what I've been reading, everything fits. Even the memory loss." She sat down on the bed, setting the open book beside her. "And I was afraid of you. At first. Sort of. After I figured out you weren't a hologram."

The ghost slid across the floor and peered at the open book.

It seemed to shrink, growing dimmer, as the idea sunk in. Then it brightened. "Does that mean you know who I am?" It asked with so much hope that Mirabella hesitated, not wanting to disappoint it.

"No," she said, finally. "No, I don't."

"Oh." The apparition became an indistinct gray mass that barely hovered above the floor.

"I really am sorry." Mirabella let the heavy book fall shut with a slap.

"As am I," the voice whispered, faint and distant, as the fuzzy blur disappeared.

A sad chill filled the room. Mirabella had thought that researching about ghosts would be fun and keep her mind off not being able to do any experiments. But now the poor thing seemed really upset. Mirabella wanted to help. Only, what could she do for someone who wasn't actually there?

This would require extensive investigation.

CHAPTER ELEVEN

"It's an invitation," Erin said, flicking her long braid over her shoulder. "For a sleepover at my house next Saturday." She waved something pink in front of Mirabella.

Mirabella shifted her bag from her left shoulder to the right one before taking the envelope. "For me?"

It had to be some kind of trick. Ever since the library, Erin and Stacey had giggled every time they saw her, but neither of the girls had even said hello to her.

"Well, yeah, for you. Duh! Why would I give it to you, if it was for somebody else?" Erin said.

A locker slammed shut behind her and Mirabella jumped.

"Go ahead. Open it," Erin said, flashing her most cutesy grin.

The envelope shook in Mirabella's hand and she glanced around. Stacey had to be watching, waiting for Mirabella to fall into the trap. Classrooms emptied and a jumble of kids swarmed by heading for the exit. Stacey was nowhere in sight.

Mirabella slid the pink polka-dotted card out of the envelope and opened it. It actually was an invitation for a sleepover.

At Erin's house.

This coming Saturday.

Mirabella whipped the envelope over and saw her name written in big loopy letters.

"See? I told you it was for you."

Mirabella shook her head in disbelief.

Erin pouted at her. "Don't you want to come?"

It could still be a trick. "I don't know if I can," Mirabella said uncertainly.

"It'll be fun. I promise." Erin shot her a broad smile.

"I'll, um, I'll have to ask my mom." Mirabella tried not to sound excited, but her heart bounced around in her chest like a crazed volleyball.

Erin was inviting her over.

To her house.

For a sleepover!

CHAPTER TWELVE

When Mirabella got home from the library, her mother was in the kitchen, making dinner. The kitchen smelled of fresh baked bread and the stew that simmered on the stove gave off the rich aroma of lentils and spices.

"Yum! That smells good." Mirabella wiped her feet on the entry mat and hung her coat on a hook. She hadn't realized how hungry she was on the way home, but the scent of the food made her stomach growl like a ravenous tiger.

"Well, the bread is the kind you buy in the store, ready to bake," her mother said. "But the lentil stew is my special recipe." She hummed a tune while she stirred the pot.

Mirabella dropped her books on a chair. She stood beside her mother and gazed at the stew, her mouth watering.

"So, tell me about your day."

"What about it?" Mirabella inhaled the spicy scent.

"Did you make any new friends?" her mother asked without turning to look at her.

"No." Mirabella frowned, grabbed her books and headed for the hall stairs.

"The correct answer is yes," her mother called after her.

Mirabella stopped half way up the staircase. "Yes?"

"That's right," her mother stood in the kitchen doorway, wearing a shiny smile. Her face glowed rosy from the warmth of the stove. "Mira, you didn't have to be afraid to ask. I'm just so glad you've finally made a friend here."

"A friend?" Mirabella turned and took a step back down the stairs. What was her mother talking about?

"And I checked with some of my coworkers. Erin Anderson is from a good family. Her parents own a well-respected construction business. Her mother and I had a nice talk on the phone today. So, while the normal rule is that I have to meet at least one of the parents in person before you can spend time at someone's house, I'm going to make an exception."

"Oh?" Her mother was making an exception because Erin's mom had called and talked to her? "Oh!" With a start, Mirabella remembered the polka-dot covered envelope she'd stashed at the bottom of her messenger bag.

"But just this once." Her mom wagged a finger. "And only because you've been so good about keeping your word and not pulling any more of your pr—experiments." She smiled.

Mirabella stood on the stairs, frozen. An icy fear mixed with giddy excitement skittered around in her stomach and she felt dizzy. Why was her mother pushing her to go to Erin's house?

She gripped the banister until her hand shook. Didn't her mother know she didn't want to go to Erin's stupid house? Why didn't she see that? She never listened to anything Mirabella said!

Her hand hurt and she relaxed her grip. A friend, her

mother had said. Could it really be true? Had she finally made a real friend here?

Her mother stood in the kitchen doorway, peering at Mirabella. "Are you feeling all right?" she asked. "You look pale."

"I'm fine, Mom."

"Get washed up and set the table, then," her mother told her. "Dinner will be ready in five minutes."

Mirabella turned and ran up to her room, her school bag thumping on the stairs behind her. Saturday was both too far away and not far enough.

CHAPTER THIRTEEN

"I've been invited to someone's house." Mirabella sprawled on her bed, surrounded by a pile of books. She spoke to the air, not knowing if the ghost could hear her, but needing to talk to someone. She knew what her mother would say, had already said at dinner. That it was good to make new friends. That to get a friend you had to be a friend. And how happy she was that Mirabella was "adjusting." But Mirabella wanted to talk, really talk to someone about it, and have someone actually listen to her feelings, not just tell her how happy they were for her.

As gloomy as it always seemed to be, the ghost was at least a good listener. And while the gauzy specter couldn't give Mirabella any real advice, at least it never tried to tell her how she should feel, or act.

If only her father were here. He'd always listened to her, no matter what she talked about. He never just nodded or said uh-huh like most grownups. Like her mom.

"For tea?" The question seemed to come from the air, but a glance in the vanity mirror showed a hazy figure sitting in the overstuffed chair in the corner of the room.

"What?" Mirabella stared at the ghost in the mirror.

"You said you'd been invited to someone's house, but not why, or by whom."

"It's a sleepover. It's at Erin Anderson's house."

"You don't sound very happy about it." The ghost seemed to be staring back at Mirabella, but its face and eyes were too blurry to tell for sure. "Don't girls your age enjoy slumber parties?"

"I don't really know her. She's just someone at school." Mirabella wondered how the ghost could see without eyes. Then again, how could it talk without vocal chords, or a tongue? She sat up so that her reflection in the mirror was superimposed over the ghost's. It was weird to see her face on the body of the ghost.

"Do you talk to any other, um, people like you?" she asked.

"Like me?"

"I mean, if someone wanted to talk to someone. Someone who was, you know, a spirit. Could you do that?"

The ghost swayed a little, as if thinking of rising, but settled back into the chair. "You're the only person I can recall speaking to, since . . . before."

"So, you don't have any friends?"

"Only you." Mirabella felt an unexpected rush of warmth at the thought that she and the ghost had actually become friends. Too bad she couldn't tell her mother she already had a friend. Then, she wouldn't have to go to the sleepover.

"Do you have many friends at school?"

Mirabella shrugged. "Not here," she said, after thinking about it. "Not anywhere, I guess."

"Don't you want to have friends?"

"It isn't that," Mirabella shot back. "It's just that I haven't had a chance to run any ex—to get to know anyone very well."

"Wouldn't a slumber party be a good way to get to know someone?"

"I suppose." Mirabella sat up and gathered the books that lay scattered across her bed.

The ghost floated up from the chair and drifted across the room. "What are you reading?"

"It's research." Mirabella glanced over her shoulder at the floating form, still wondering how it could see or speak.

"Homework?"

"Not really. It's mostly stuff about you."

The ghost hovered beside the bed, leaning forward and read some of the titles aloud. "Ghost Hunter; What Haunts the Living; Haunts, Spirits and Sprites." It turned to Mirabella. "These are about me?"

"Not you specifically," Mirabella said. She was surprised that the ghost could read. But, she supposed, reading was probably something she'd remember for a long time too, if she were a ghost. Maybe forever. She gazed at the comforting pile of books. "And some of the things I've read are pretty unrealistic. But there are some things in here that make a lot of sense."

"Such as?" The ghost settled to the floor and waited expectantly.

"The stuff about how ghosts are attached to houses or places that are meaningful to them. We just have to figure out why you're attached to this house." She glanced up to gauge the ghost's reaction to this information, and thought she could read a frown in its face. She rushed on. "That they can lose their memories. And we know that's true."

The ghost nodded in agreement.

"The same author says that the reason they—spirits, I

mean—stay attached is because they have unfinished business with the living. And that you—I mean, they—can only move on after their business is complete."

"So, I'm stuck here?" The ghost began to flicker.

"Not if we can find out why you're here and I can help you take care of your unfinished business," Mirabella said, hopefully.

"Oh, and there's something I've been wanting to ask you." Mirabella held out her father's copy of *A Fine and Private Place*, by Peter S. Beagle, the pages worn from constant rereading. She pointed to a sentence marked with yellow highlighter. "What does this mean?"

The ghost drifted nearer. "The dead have nothing to do with dandelions, and the dead don't make wishes." The ghost's quavery voice faded to a whisper on the last word.

A ripple ran through its translucent form. Its wispy face wrinkled like a crumpled sheet of tissue paper, and it rose abruptly into the air. "I don't know!" it said, drifting toward the closet. "Why do you ask me these things?"

Mirabella closed the book and hugged it to her. "I'm sorry. I didn't mean to upset you. I just thought you could explain it to me."

"Explain it? How can I explain it, when I don't know anything? When I can't even remember my own name?" The room vibrated as the ghost's voice grew louder, a resonating moan like the groaning pipes in the old apartment building where Mirabella and her mother used to live. What if that had been ghosts, too, and not just old water pipes like everyone thought?

The ghost wavered for a moment. "I can't help but wonder if you are merely unthoughtful or purposely cruel." It flickered like a wind-blown candle, then disappeared.

CHAPTER FOURTEEN

The school hallway emptied and the second buzzer sounded. Mirabella scooted into the classroom and slid into her seat, just as Mrs. Flizzer opened her attendance book. She glanced around while the teacher called the students' names and checked each of them off as present or absent. Erin wasn't in class today, so she wouldn't have to RSVP on the invitation. Mirabella's insides bounced like a kid on a trampoline. Her normal sense of relief at not having to do something she didn't want to was twisted by a strong feeling of disappointment.

Weird.

Mirabella put her elbows on the desk and cupped her chin in her hands. Had she actually wanted to spend the night at Erin's house?

"Polidoro. Mirabella Polidoro!"

She sat up straight and jerked her hand into the air. "Present!"

Someone behind her whispered something and a snicker of

laughter pierced her between the shoulder blades. Great. One more stupid reason for them to laugh at her. Now they'd be saying she didn't even know her own name. She wanted to melt through the floor. It made her envy the way the ghost could just disappear anytime it didn't like what was happening.

What would it be like to just flicker and go out like that? It didn't seem to be painful. At least, the ghost never complained about it. With a start, she realized she was doing it again, daydreaming while she should be paying attention.

She took out her notebook and tried to concentrate on what Mrs. Flizzer was saying, but school was totally boring. None of the teachers taught anything interesting, like haunted houses or holograms. The closest thing to an experiment that she'd gotten to do in her 4th period Science class was to rub balloons on different surfaces to see how long they would stick to a wall. Then, based on how long the balloons took to fall off the wall, Mr. Haley had them rate the surfaces in the order of how much static they built up. It wasn't rocket science. Not even close.

The rest of the period seemed like a hundred and fifty years long. And at the end of class, Mirabella looked down to find her notebook filled with words and ideas she didn't recall having heard or thought. She tried to read what she'd written, but the sentences were muddled and a lot of the words didn't make sense. Great. She was becoming as forgetful as the ghost that haunted Aunt Clovinia's house.

As she shoved the notebook into her bag and heaved it up onto her shoulder, her pen rolled off the desk and onto the floor. She leaned over to grab it, using the desk to keep herself from tumbling over from the weight and wondered, not for the first time, why she carried around so many books and things. Her mother kept telling her she was going to have back problems from it, but she just couldn't seem to leave the house without a ton of stuff.

She grasped her pen and thought about the poor ghost, who spent day after day, year after year, empty-handed and alone, with nothing to do but wander through Aunt Clovinia's drafty old house. She wondered if Aunt Clovinia believed in ghosts, then remembered that none of the adults she knew or had ever known, aside from G'ma Marita, had believed in any kind of spirits.

Her mother believed in science and medicine. Aunt Clovinia, who had been an executive assistant to a bank president was fond of saying, "business and commerce keep the world from collapsing." Mirabella didn't think that was right. She was sure it was actually some kind of scientific principle that kept the world from collapsing, not business. And certainly not commerce, whatever that was.

She suddenly realized that she had no idea whether or not her father had believed in spirits or ghosts. She couldn't remember him saying. But he'd always been extra nice to G'ma Marita.

CHAPTER FIFTEEN

It was odd to see the ghost staring out of the bedroom window, as if it were a regular person watching the rain fall from the sidewalk-colored sky. It made Mirabella sad to see it look so forlorn. The ghost reached out and traced its finger in the air as if it were writing something in the beaded moisture that fogged the narrow window.

Mirabella thought about the movies she'd seen where people caught glimpses of shadows moving in the windows of spooky, old houses. "Why don't other people see you?" she asked.

The filmy figure tilted its head. "I don't know," it whispered. "Perhaps because they don't want to. Perhaps, like ghosts and dandelions, most people have nothing to do with the dead. Although, I think I would make wishes, if I could recall who I had been in life."

"Where do you go?" Mirabella abruptly changed the subject.

"Hmmmm?" The ghost continued to stare out the window at the drizzling sky.

"Where do you go?" Mirabella asked again.

"Where do I go?"

"Yeah. When you pop out of sight. Is there somewhere special that you go?"

"Somewhere special?"

"Yes." Mirabella walked over and stood beside the ghost. She stared out the window, searching for a speck of blue sky among the dirty-looking clouds. "You know," she finally said in a quiet voice. "Someplace where you feel safe, where no one can bother you or tell you what to do. A place that's yours and no one else's." She stared at the fog-misted window, wishing she could see what the ghost had been writing, but the gauzy finger hadn't made so much as a smudge in the haze that clung to the glass. "Like when I read, it takes me to special worlds where I can get lost in the adventure and, you know, forget about . . . things for a while."

She raised her hand toward the window, paused and glanced at the ghost's blurry outline. It must be horrible to exist without being able to touch anything. To spend years not being able to go anywhere or do more than move really small objects. It would be worse than being in prison. Mirabella shivered. She put her finger to the window and felt a tendril of relief that it was cold to her touch, and that she could trace the shape of a teardrop on the glass.

"I'm not sure." The ghost sounded confused. "Sometimes I find myself outside, but I don't always know how I got there. And I can't go beyond the edge of the property." It lifted a hand to the teardrop outlined in the moisture. "But sometimes I just find myself sitting in a corner of the attic and I don't remember how I got there. It's like I fell asleep and woke up there, or maybe walked there in my sleep."

"That's terrible." Mirabella shook her head.

"I suppose this whole house is my special place," the ghost said with a low sigh. "At least, that's what your research seems to suggest. But don't you think it seems odd?"

"What?"

"That anyone would choose to trap themselves somewhere and then forget why."

"I suppose, " Mirabella said. "But do you really think you made a conscious choice to stay here? Or do you think it just sort of happened because you weren't ready to leave at first, and then . . . after a while . . . you just couldn't?"

"I wish I knew." The ghost floated away from the window. "I truly wish I knew."

Mirabella thought it must not have been a conscious choice for the ghost to become trapped in the old house. Then again, it might not have been so old at the time. It might have been a really nice house once, but time and weather had worried at it, loosening its nails and boards.

She stared at the bedroom floor, which was solid wood cut in wide planks. The old varnish hadn't been completely worn away in some places and she could see what it might have looked like all shiny new and polished. It had probably been nice and sturdy when it was first built and wouldn't have creaked and groaned like it did now.

Someone had built the house to be a home. Maybe a place to raise kids. There were enough rooms for a big family. Or lots of guests. But the years had worn off the newness. Now, it was just a dusty old house.

As if to remind her of how dusty, Mirabella's nose twitched. She tried to grab a tissue, but too late. She let go a sneeze that jerked her head down hard. The ghost, who had been hovering a short distance away, blew across the room like a sheet of paper caught in a windstorm and faded through the wall.

Mirabella started to call out an apology, but a string of smaller sneezes hit her one after the other. "I can't ibagine anyone choosing to be trapped forebber in a house like this," she complained, wiping at her tender nose.

CHAPTER SIXTEEN

Mirabella's stomach twisted into a double knot. She hadn't known Stacey would be staying the night at Erin's house, too. But her mother had already driven away, the old minivan coughing out a cloud of smoke the size of an elephant before sputtering around the corner. It was too late to go home, now.

Erin led her up the stairs to her room, talking and giggling the whole way, while Stacey trailed behind them. Mirabella glanced over her shoulder at the dark-haired girl, who seemed to take pleasure in tormenting her at every turn. Stacey smiled at her and Mirabella nearly tripped on the stairs.

"Are you okay?" Erin asked.

"Sure," Mirabella lied. "My shoelace is just loose, that's all." She let her messenger bag slide to the floor and dropped to one knee, making a show of retying her shoe.

Stacey waited on the stairs until she was finished, then the two girls followed Erin into her bedroom. The room was as large as the one Mirabella slept in at Aunt Clovinia's house, but unlike Mirabella's room it was bright and filled with shiny new furniture. The large canopied bed stretched out into the room like a big pink tongue. The walls were painted white with wide magenta stripes and the floor was covered with bright pink carpet so thick Mirabella's feet sank into it with every step. An impressive computer system sparkled on the full size desk. There were no books, but shelves filled with porcelain dolls and stuffed animals reached to the ceiling.

"You can put your stuff over there on the big chair," Erin said. "My dad will set up the air mattresses later. Did you bring your sleeping bag?"

Mirabella felt her face redden and she turned away, gingerly placing her overnight bag on the chair Erin had indicated. "I don't have a sleeping bag," she said.

"That's okay," Erin shrugged. "My mom has lots of extra blankets. And pillows," she added, eyeing Mirabella's small bag.

Stacey flopped onto the bed. "So, what are we going to do first?" she asked.

"We could check out Jacob47's MyPage. He always posts new pictures on the weekend. And he is so hawt!"

"We could," said Stacey. "But I think we should ask Marbles what she wants to do." She smiled brightly.

Marbles. There it was. Mirabella pursed her lips together and tried not to frown. This was a stupid idea. She shouldn't have come here. She knew it was a set-up. *Stupid. Stupid. Stupid.* "Um, whatever you want to do is fine." She forced herself to smile back at Stacey. No way was she going to let Stacey see that the name bothered her.

"We could always play 'Secrets.'" Erin raised her shoulders and eyebrows at the same time in one of her cutesy shrugs.

"What a great idea," Stacey said. She hopped onto the bed

and sat cross-legged. Her mint green socks matched her shirt and headband perfectly. "But you have to go first this time."

"Oh, all right," Erin rolled her eyes and kneeled on the bed.

The two girls watched Mirabella with expectant faces. She hesitated, her feet sunk deep into the thick carpet. She wasn't sure what kind of game they wanted to play, but she was certain it wouldn't be any fun with Stacey around.

"Come on," Erin said, patting the bed beside her. "You have to sit up here where we can whisper. But take off your shoes first." She glanced at Mirabella's raggedy tennis shoes.

Mirabella bent down and struggled to untie her shoelaces. Her fingers shook and the knots seemed to be glued together. Why had she double-knotted them out on the stairs just now?

"We could have some music, at least." Erin leaped up and clicked a few keys on her computer keyboard. Music spilled from overhead.

Mirabella glanced up at the speakers embedded in the ceiling and Erin followed her gaze.

"My dad had them installed. Aren't they cool? They're even connected to the surround sound on the TV. Wait till you hear what "Disco Dance Party" sounds like on them." She pointed to the big flat screen TV on the far wall. "It makes it seem like you're in a real dance club."

"Yeah, it's great," Stacey said, giving Erin a look. "But what's really cool, is turning out all the lights and watching "slice and dice" movies. Talk about creepy!" She opened her eyes wide.

"Slice and dice?" Mirabella said.

"You know, totally scary horror movies. With tons of blood." Stacey made a screeching sound and a stabbing motion with her arm.

"Come on," Erin said. "We can always watch a movie. Right now, let's do a few rounds of 'Secrets.'"

Her shoes finally untied, Mirabella slipped them off and set them next to the chair that held her things. Then she slid carefully onto the bed and sat on her feet so her mismatched socks wouldn't show. "What do we do now?" she asked.

Erin gaped at her. "Haven't you ever played 'Secrets?'"

Mirabella shook her head weakly.

"That's okay," Stacey told her, giving Erin a funny look. "It's easy. You just have to share something about yourself that the other players don't already know. It gets harder when you've been friends with someone forever, like Erin and me. Right?"

"Right." Erin lowered her voice to a whisper. "And then you have to tell real secrets."

Stacey nodded. "But it'll be easy for you this time, 'cause we don't know you that good."

"And it'll help us get to know you better," Erin added, her voice rising in that cutesy way she seemed to do everything.

Mirabella eyed them both, uncomfortably. Erin seemed okay, but getting to know Stacey didn't sound like much fun. And sharing any kind of secret with her seemed like a bad idea. But there were lots of things these girls didn't know about her that weren't really secrets. Or, at least weren't important. What could it hurt?

CHAPTER SEVENTEEN

"Well?" Stacey waggled her head at Erin.

Erin made an ouch-filled face. "Last week, I borrowed my mom's razor and shaved my legs," she whispered.

"Prove it." Stacey twisted her mouth up and squinted at Erin.

Pulling up the leg of her brand new jeans, Erin showed them a fresh scab that ran down the length of her shin. "I guess I didn't use enough cream or something." She made a frowny face.

"Did it bleed much?" Mirabella asked, staring at the dark reddish brown patch that covered the front of Erin's leg.

"Yeee-ah," Erin drawled. "I practically used a whole roll of T.P. to soak it up."

"Yuck!" Stacey grimaced.

"And it stung like crazy! It was all I could do not to scream."

"But you didn't?" Mirabella wished she had her journal so

she could take notes.

"No, duh. I didn't want my mom to find out I was messing with her stuff." Erin pulled her pant leg back down. "Luckily, I haven't had to dress up for anything. Of course, since it's so wintery out, I suppose I could wear tights or leggings under a skirt if I had to." She rubbed at the front of her leg through her jeans.

"Enough of the gross." Stacey bounced up and down on the bed, grinning like a crazy car salesman on a late night TV commercial. "It's my turn."

Erin stopped rubbing her leg. "You look like you're dying to tell the biggest best secret in the universe."

Stacey nodded and kept bouncing.

"What is it?" Erin tilted her head to one side. "Did you? No! You didn't! Did you?"

"Yesss!" Stacey squealed.

Erin screeched and started bouncing with her. The bed rocked and swayed, nearly tumbling Mirabella onto the floor. She grabbed up a handful of bedspread while the other two girls continued to squeal and jounce up and down.

"I can't believe you did it."

"Me neither."

"Did what?" Mirabella blurted.

The two girls giggled and blushed. Finally, they shushed each other and leaned in toward Mirabella, their heads almost touching hers.

"I kissed Derek Sanders." Stacey gave Erin a wide-eyed look and grinned, showing her perfect teeth.

Erin rocked back, covered her mouth with her hands, and shook her head back and forth.

"On the lips." Stacey gave Mirabella a dark mischievous look. "We made out for like an hour."

The two girls bounced and squealed some more. This time

Mirabella hung on to the bedpost with both hands until the rollicking subsided. "You kissed a boy on the mouth for an hour?" she asked in amazement.

"Well, he kissed me first." Stacey pinched her lips together. "But then I kissed him back. And then, well . . ." The bouncing and shrieking started up again.

Mirabella waited for the new episode of squealing to stop. After what seemed like forever, the girls calmed down, and Stacey studied Mirabella for a moment. "What's the matter?" she asked. "Don't you like boys?"

Mirabella wondered what the correct answer should be. She hadn't really thought about it before.

Erin put her hand to the side of her face. "That's right," she said. "You don't know who Derek is."

"Oooooh." Stacy stage-swooned. "He's only the cutest boy who ever attended JFE."

"He is sooooo cute," Erin said with a long sigh.

"And he only lives in the biggest most expensive house in town."

"Is he in any of our classes?" Mirabella asked.

"Derek? In our classes?" Erin giggled. "No way! He doesn't even go to JFE anymore."

"He's in Junior High already," Stacey said, tossing her hair back from her face.

"Oh." Mirabella tried not to sound too surprised.

"You have to tell us all about it!" Erin said.

"Well, my parents know his parents really well," Stacey said. "And we got invited over for their big Fall Bash." She looked down her nose at Mirabella. "That's an annual party they have every year. They have people come in and decorate the whole place and there's always a live band and the food is all catered."

Erin rolled her eyes. "Get to the good part."

"Well, all the adults stay upstairs and talk and do completely boring stuff and the kids get to have their own party in the basement where they have a game room and a movie theater with a popcorn machine and everything. And we were in the theater room, in the dark, watching a really gruesome slasher movie called *Gore* or something. And Derek leaned over and he put his arm around my shoulder." Stacey paused dramatically. "And . . . then . . . he kissed me. And then the next thing, we were kind of tangled up and there was a whole lot of hot stuff happening."

More giggling and bouncing ensued.

Mirabella tried to be excited with them, but all she could manage was a big fake smile that hurt her cheeks.

"There's no secret I can think of bigger than that!" Erin said when they'd finally settled down.

"I know," Stacey said. "But I'm trusting you both with it, so it had better stay a secret. Right?" Her mean-spirited glare suggested terrible things would happen if Mirabella breathed a word to anyone.

"Right," Mirabella said, nodding.

"No problem," Erin said. "But are you sure Derek won't say anything?"

"Derek is a gentleman," Stacey said. "He won't say anything."

"Your turn," Erin said.

Two sets of eyes bored into Mirabella and she wanted to run home and hide in her room. She turned away and picked at a loose thread on the sleeve of her sweater. "I don't have any secrets as big as either of yours," she mumbled.

"That's all right," Erin said. "It doesn't have to be as huge as that."

"Of course not," Stacey chimed in. "It can be as simple as, I don't know, say wetting the bed."

"Wetting the bed?" Mirabella said, jerking her head up to look at Stacey. "At our age?"

A look of worry fluttered across Erin's face. "She didn't mean you," she said, quickly. "She just used that as an example." She nudged the other girl on the shoulder. "Didn't you?"

"Sure," Stacey told her. "I just meant it didn't have to be earth-shattering. Just, you know, something personal."

"Hmmm," Mirabella scrunched up her face in thought. She wasn't comfortable sharing personal things. Not with someone she hardly knew. And especially not with Stacey, who she still didn't like.

But Erin was being so nice to her, and Stacey was at least talking to her, almost like they were friends. And would she have told her about being kissed by a boy, if she didn't trust her to keep it a secret? Although, it wasn't like there was anyone for Mirabella to tell. It wasn't like she had any friends here. Maybe, just maybe, if she told them something personal about herself, some little secret, it would help them all be friends.

Her eyes flicked back and forth between the two girls, who sat waiting. Waiting for her to say something, to share something, to let them know she wanted to be their friend, too.

"I like to do psychological experiments," she whispered.

CHAPTER EIGHTEEN

"So, you play tricks on people and watch what they do and then you write it down?" Erin's face wrinkled into a question.

"I record their reactions," Mirabella corrected her. "And they're not tricks. They're psychological experiments. Although, my mom calls them pranks. But you know how adults are. They really don't understand anything. Right?"

Stacey leaned back on the pillows heaped against the headboard. "Could you give us an example of one of these experiments?"

Mirabella thought for a minute. "Once, where we used to live, I colored the neighbor's cat dark blue with orange stripes."

"I bet that got a big reaction," Erin said, raising her eyebrows.

"Not at first." Mirabella bit the inside of her mouth before continuing. "The neighbor was a big football fan and it turned out that those were his favorite team's colors. So, at first he thought one of his friends did it to be funny. But I didn't use waterproof coloring and, a couple of days later, the neighbor let his cat outside, which normally would've been fine, you know? Only, it was raining." Mirabella almost cringed remembering how mad her mother had been when the neighbor showed her his carpet.

"Oh, wow," Erin giggled.

"It wouldn't have been so bad," Mirabella told them. "But he'd just had his old carpet replaced with a real expensive wool kind."

"Was it a really light color?" Stacey asked, a large grin stretching across her face.

"Yeah. He was super mad." Mirabella hung her head and studied her fingertips.

Erin and Stacey broke out laughing and the bed began to wriggle and shake.

"That is so cool," Stacey said, gasping for breath.

Surprised, Mirabella looked up at them. The neighbor certainly hadn't thought it was cool, or funny, to have bright-colored paw prints across his entire floor. Her mother hadn't been amused. Especially, when she'd had to pay to have the carpet professionally cleaned. But these girls seemed to think it was just about the funniest thing they'd ever heard. Although, it was kind of funny to think about now. A smile forced the corners of her mouth up and she started to laugh.

"Excuse me." Erin said. She sat up straight, stuck her nose in the air and looked down it at the other girls, trying to keep a straight face. "Do you have any paw-print curtains to match my floor?" She grabbed her stomach and doubled over.

Stacey waved her hand at them. "Oh, stop!" she said. "Before I pee my pants!"

"He had a calico carpet," Mirabella said.

The other girls stopped laughing, their faces crinkled with

confusion. Then they seemed to get the joke, and they both fell back on the bed, whooping in hysterics.

Stacey gasped, trying to catch her breath. Then she hiccoughed and threw a glance at Erin. "So, what kind of experiments do you think would work at school?"

CHAPTER NINETEEN

"How was the sleepover?" her mother asked, setting the laundry basket on the kitchen table. She pulled out a scrub shirt printed with bright butterflies, flapped out the wrinkles with a snap, and hung it on a hanger. She had a lot of different nursing scrubs. Some even had matching pants. But she mostly had a lot of plain-colored pants and printed shirts that she could mix and match. She said that way it didn't feel like she was always wearing the same thing to work.

"It was okay," Mirabella said. She yawned, stretching her arms high above her head. She'd hardly slept at all at Erin's last night. Between the soda and junk food, and all the laughing and the video games, she'd had way too much energy.

She'd totally sucked at Disco Dance Party, or as Stacey and Erin called it, "DDP." She'd mostly watched Stacey and Erin "rock the night away to the coolest disco hits." That's what the announcer kept saying in between songs. And Erin and Stacey always said it with him. It was obvious they'd spent tons of time playing the game. They were both really good at it.

"Only okay?" Her mother shook out another scrub shirt, this one covered in pastel flowers, before hanging it up beside the first one. "You look like you didn't get much sleep. Seems to me that means it must have been more than just okay." She raised her eyebrows.

"I guess we did stay up kind of late." Mirabella opened the refrigerator and stared at the contents.

"Doing what?" Her mother finished hanging the last of her shirts and started pulling out socks and laying them out on the table in matched pairs.

"We played video games and watched movies," Mirabella said. She closed the refrigerator and rummaged through the kitchen cabinets, searching for something to eat.

"And her parents didn't mind you staying up so late?"

"Erin has a flat screen TV on her bedroom wall. So, it didn't really bother anyone else, I don't think." She pulled a jar of peanut butter from the cupboard.

"Does Erin have any siblings?" Her mother took apart two sets of dark blue socks and held them up to the light.

"She has a brother," Mirabella said, opening the loaf of bread. "But he's a lot older than she is. I think he's away at college or something. Do we have any bananas left?"

"Behind you." Her mother pointed. "In the hanging basket."

Mirabella slathered two pieces of bread with peanut butter, and peeled and cut the banana, dropping the thick slices onto one of the pieces of peanut butter-covered bread. Then she smashed the other slice of bread on top and took a huge bite. She chewed slowly, working the peanut butter from her teeth and gums before swallowing.

"There's milk," her mother offered.

"I'd rather have apple juice," Mirabella said, her words

suddenly thick from more than peanut butter and banana. Her father had taught her to make peanut butter and banana sandwiches. He'd always made faces with the banana slices. Mirabella would squish on the tops of the sandwiches while her dad poured large glasses of apple juice for them to wash down their sticky-gooey sandwiches. She really missed him.

"Sorry," her mother said, grabbing the hangers of clothes and heading upstairs with them. "We're fresh out."

Mirabella sat staring at her sandwich. The memory of her father's accident squeezed her chest and constricted her throat. It was like her mother didn't even care. How could she not care? An angry swarm of bees roiled in Mirabella's stomach where the humongous hunger had been just moments before. Keeping an eye out for her mother, she dumped the rest of the sandwich into the garbage can and covered it with her napkin.

CHAPTER TWENTY

A chill air filled her bedroom and Mirabella blew out her breath to see if it was cold enough to make a cloud. Nope. It just felt like it. She rummaged through the dilapidated dresser and pulled on a sweater before plopping in front of the vanity. The only items sitting on its glossy surface were her hairbrush and comb, and the framed picture of her with her dad at the county fair.

In the photo, they were standing in front of one of those safari scenes, her father pretending to hold open the jaws of a huge stuffed lion while sticking his head inside its mouth. She had the lion's tail gripped in her fists, pretending to strain at holding the lion back. They were both mugging for the camera.

That fair was one of her favorite memories aside from the nights they'd spent staring up at the sky. She thought back to those nights, how he'd tell her the names of the stars and constellations, and how she would repeat them back to him. There were no photographs of those times. But every night she had the stars in the sky to remind her.

"Vega, Deneb, Altair," she recited under her breath, closing her eyes and envisioning the speckles of light shimmering in the dark. "Draw a line in the air, from Vega to Arcturus and find Hercules the Giant there." She paused, bringing the constellations into focus in the imaginary sky on the insides of her eyelids. "His torso is the Keystone, four stars in all. Standing on his head, he never tips or falls. Head to head with Draco, the dragon of the skies. Between the Big and Little Dippers, Draco forever flies."

She pulled her hands up into her sleeves, wrapping the sweater closer around her body to get warm. Something tickled her cheek, but when she reached up it felt like she'd plunged her hand into a vat of ice water and she jolted up with a startled yelp.

"Sorry," came a whispery voice. "I didn't mean to disturb you. I just wanted to hear what you were saying."

The ghost drifted closer and Mirabella shivered.

"What was it?" the filmy figure asked.

"What was what?" Mirabella tried to focus on the wavering features of the ghost's face.

"The poem you were reciting." The ghost tilted to one side, then swayed back to its former position.

"It was a . . ." Mirabella fumbled for the word. "You know. A way to remember. A rhyme to help your memory." She twisted the sweater tighter, hugging herself. "A something device."

"A mnemonic device?" The ghost asked.

"Yes! That's it." Mirabella said. "Wait. How did you know that?"

"I—I'm not sure." The ghost wavered.

"Don't go," Mirabella whispered.

"But how did I know that?" The ghost's voice was filled

with pain. "How can I recall some obscure idea like that, but not know my own name?"

"Maybe the word has some meaning for you," Mirabella said, "other than the definition."

"What do you mean?"

"Well, suppose it has something to do with who you are. Like maybe you used to be an actress who had to memorize a lot of lines for a play or something. Then you'd probably know something about mnemonic devices, right?"

"Perhaps." The ghost was slow to respond, uncertainty coloring its voice. "But there could be a hundred reasons for knowing that, couldn't there?"

Mirabella squeezed the ends of her sweater sleeves in her fists. "I suppose," she said. "But what if memorization has something to do with who you are?"

"You mean learning by rote?"

"Learning by what?" Mirabella asked.

"By rote," the ghost explained. "It means learning something by memorizing it, rather than understanding it. Like certain math formulas."

"Right," Mirabella said. "So, you seem to know about mnemonic devices and learning by rote. What else do you know about remembering?"

"You mean besides the fact that I can't?" the ghost snapped at her, and then it began to blink.

"Please, don't do that." Mirabella pleaded.

"Do what?"

"Blink out and disappear. You always do that when you get upset."

"I do?"

"Yeah," Mirabella said, pointing a sweater-covered hand at the apparition. "Look."

The ghost peered down at itself and the blinking stopped.

"I'm sorry. I hadn't realized." Sadness clung to its words.

"It's okay." Mirabella tried to sound reassuring. "I mean, I understand. Sometimes, when I get mad my mind fades in and out and I feel like my whole body is blinking like that, and I can't understand what my mom is saying. It's like I can only hear some of the words, like my ears are blinking, too." Mirabella caught herself frowning and offered the ghost her most supportive smile. "Only, as much as I sometimes want to, I never actually disappear like you do."

"I don't do it on purpose," the ghost said in a quavery voice, pulsing a little around the edges. "When I get upset, I just seem to find myself somewhere else. And I don't always remember how I got there, or where I was just the moment before."

"So, even though it might sound like a nice idea to be able to disappear when you're upset or in trouble, I guess it isn't such a good thing," Mirabella said.

"Not really." The ghost stretched up tall and thin, then shrank back down, settling into its usual appearance, like someone stretching and taking a deep breath before letting it out again. It reminded Mirabella of the way her father used to stand and stretch after lying on his back and staring up at the stars. Standing and stretching had been his signal for her to go to bed. But she'd lie there in the darkness, watching his silhouette show against the sugar-dusted sky and wait for him to tell her, "*Mirabella, il mio bel cuore, cronometrare per il letto.*" She loved to hear him say the words in Italian, but she loved even more knowing what they meant. "Mirabella, my beautiful heart, time for bed." She let out a sigh.

"Was it something I said?" the ghost asked in a soft voice.

"What?" Mirabella blinked, jolted back to the drafty room in the old house.

"You're sad again," the wispy figure said.

Mirabella's throat tightened. "I'm okay," she said, knowing she wasn't very convincing.

She forced herself to sound more cheerful. "Maybe we can help you remember some new things," she said. "You seem really good with words. Maybe we could play a word association game."

Mirabella and her father had played lots of word games, but the word association game was the one she liked the best because her father always picked the wackiest words to go with the most normal ones. By the time they'd played for only a few minutes they would both be laughing so hard they'd have trouble catching their breath. Even if the ghost didn't really remember anything, Mirabella thought, maybe she could make it feel happy for a little while.

The ghost hesitated.

"It can't really hurt, can it?"

"I suppose we could try," the ghost said, uncertainly.

"Okay." Mirabella charged on. "I'll say a word and then you say the first thing that comes into your head. She paused for a moment. "Words."

"Words?"

"You're not supposed to repeat what I said. You're supposed to say the first new word that comes to you."

"Yes, yes. Of course." The ghost turned a lighter shade.

"Let's try again." Mirabella smiled in encouragement. "Black."

"White?"

"That's it," Mirabella said and wrote down the words side-by-side in her notebook.

"Bright."

"Light."

"Hot."

"Cold."

"Sun."

"Moon."

"Father."

"Mother."

Mirabella's heart hopscotched and she paused, wondering why the ghost would connect those two words. They certainly didn't go together in Mirabella's world. Not anymore. She took a breath and continued.

"Sister."

"Brother?" The word had come out as a question.

Did that mean the ghost had brothers or not? Mirabella made sure to add the question mark after the word in her notes.

"Doctor."

"Husband."

Another strange pair. Mirabella crinkled her nose. "Lawyer," she said.

"Justice," the ghost responded.

"School."

"Teacher."

"Children."

"Death."

Surprised, Mirabella looked up from her journal. "Death?"

"Oh, dear!" Without so much as a single flicker, the ghost vanished.

CHAPTER TWENTY-ONE

Mirabella peered around the chatter-filled lunchroom. Groups of kids sat at tables, eating and talking. Normally, she would stand in the doorway and search for a quiet corner where she could sit by herself. Sometimes, she'd sit at the far end of the table across from some of the younger kids, even though they ignored her like most of the kids in her classes. But today she was looking for Erin and Stacey. Now that they were friends, maybe they could sit together at lunch.

She fidgeted in the doorway, scanning faces, searching for a sign of Erin's blonde-streaked hair. She stopped at the sight of a familiar face. Stacey stared straight at her, a frown on her lips, lines wrinkling her forehead. She leaned forward and said something to the person across the table from her, who was wearing a fuzzy knit hat. The person in the hat turned. It was Erin. She waved at Mirabella.

A warm bubble of relief settled over Mirabella. She waved back and headed across the room, jostling her way between benches and tables and kids with trays. She sidestepped just in time to avoid tripping over the strap of someone's backpack. For a moment, it seemed like the entire world was between her and the table where Erin and Stacey sat.

"Hi," she said when she finally reached them.

Stacey greeted her with an odd half-smile. "Oh, hey," she said. "Too bad you couldn't get here sooner, we were just finishing." She shoved her half-eaten burger and untouched fries away from her and wiped her hands on a napkin. "But you can still sit here, if you want." Her voice was syrupy sweet.

Mirabella sat down next to Erin, spread a napkin on the table and began to unpack her lunch. She placed each item on the napkin in the order she planned to eat them. Her carrot sticks, then her sandwich, and a bag of animal crackers for dessert. She set her bottle of water on the far right corner of the napkin. Then she took out a second napkin and placed it in her lap.

Stacey cleared her throat. "You know," she said. "You could do me and Erin a really big favor."

"A favor?" Mirabella pulled out a carrot stick and took a bite.

"Sure. We're friends, aren't we?" Stacey gave her an innocent look. "And friends help each other out, right?"

"I guess so." Mirabella shrugged.

"So, how about you copy out your notes from class and give them to us?"

"Which class?" Mirabella took another bite of carrot.

"All of them."

Mirabella nearly choked on her carrot. "All of them? Why do you need the notes from all of our classes?"

Stacey chewed her lower lip. "It's just that you're so much smarter than we are," she said.

Mirabella felt her face grow red.

"So, your notes have to be way better than ours," Stacey rushed on. "We just figured that if we had your notes, it would help us to do better in class. Right, Erin?"

Erin glanced at Stacey, then nodded in agreement.

"I guess I could loan you my notes," Mirabella said.

"Yeah, that'd be great." Stacey frowned. "Except that we're so busy with, you know, extracurricular stuff. And everyone knows how a person can read their own writing so much better than anyone else, so it takes them less time to copy their notes." She pushed her hair back over her shoulder. "So, it would be a lot easi—better if you just copy them for us. I mean, if you're really our friend."

Mirabella chewed a mouthful of carrot while she thought about it. "I guess I could do that," she said, finally. "When do you need them by?"

"Tomorrow would be great." Stacey chirped.

"Tomorrow?"

"Thanks! That's excellent. You're a really good friend," Stacey said.

Mirabella opened her mouth to argue, but in a sudden rush, Stacey bounced up out of her seat, making a show of checking the clock. "Oops! We have to go." She nudged Erin, who took a last quick bite of apple and shoved the rest of her lunch back into her lunch bag. Erin scooped Stacey's leftovers onto the cafeteria tray and dumped the garbage into the trash can before stacking the tray on a pile of dirty dishes.

"See you," Stacey said to Mirabella.

Erin pursed her lips and followed Stacey out of the lunchroom.

Mirabella sat by herself, her lunch still spread out on the napkin in front of her. What had just happened? Had she just agreed to copy her notes from all their classes? What was she, a copier machine? She stared at her lunch, but it wasn't as if the animal crackers had the answers. She liked Erin, but she wasn't so sure about Stacey. Then again, would copying her notes for them be such a big deal? Especially if it meant that Erin and Stacey would let her hang out with them, maybe even be friends with her?

She toyed with the bag of carrot sticks, flattening it out and tracing the cool pieces of carrot with her fingers. Sure it would be a lot of work, but didn't her mom always tell her that being a good friend took effort, but that it was worth it? She pulled out another carrot stick and bit down, crunching it between her teeth. Besides, it was just a few pages of notes. What could it hurt?

CHAPTER TWENTY-TWO

The thick library book lay on Mirabella's bed. She opened it to the page marked with a large sticky note and sprawled before it. Chin in her hands, she read the passage aloud. "Ghosts and spirits that are attached to a specific place may only be freed from that attachment either by completion of their unfinished business with the living, or in the worst cases, exorcism. However, if the place of attachment is destroyed before either of these occurs, the spirit is doomed to walk the earth forever lost and alone, without memories or even the comfort of the knowledge of its former self to accompany it."

"That sounds terrible." A shudder ran down the ghost in misty waves.

"Are you all right?" Mirabella asked in concern.

The phantom faded momentarily, but for a change it didn't disappear, so Mirabella kept reading. "After decades of lonely wandering, such a spirit may finally dissipate. But in rare cases, the remaining trace of the spirit, which is known as a shade, may attach itself to a living individual and attempt to bond with him or her. Shades are most often drawn to innocents, that is, children or persons of less advanced intellect. Unfortunately, this type of haunting generally causes the target of the attachment to behave in a manner identified as abnormal and thus being diagnosed with a mental disease or defect, often resulting in social stigma, ostracization or institutionalization."

"No!" With a suddenness that startled her, the ghost disappeared from the chair in the corner and rematerialized on the bed next to Mirabella. "That can't be right," it said, peering over Mirabella's shoulder. "Let me see."

Mirabella wondered what it would be like to be a ghost and be able to disappear and reappear, to float and fade through walls, and haunt people. There were a few people Mirabella would love to haunt, and as a ghost she'd be able to do amazing psychological experiments. The possibilities bounced around inside her head. Instead of a recording behind the dryer, she'd be able to appear right inside it.

A loud sob brought her back from her daydreaming, or what her mother called daze-dreaming. "That's awful," the specter cried. "Those poor children!"

The giggle that had formed in Mirabella's throat stuck there at the sight of the miserable ghost. She closed the book with a thud. "What about the poor ghosts?"

"But they're the ones that cause the children to be diagnosed as mentally unstable!"

"Yes, but they don't really even know they're ghosts, do they?"

"I didn't know until you told me." The ghost shuddered, rippling like a flag in the wind. "But now, because of you, I do know. And I can't bear the idea that I might cause harm to anyone, much less a child."

"Well, that's not going to happen," Mirabella tried to

comfort the shivering figure. "It isn't like this house is going anywhere, and you have me to help you. We just have to figure out what your unfinished business is."

"Then what?" The spirit sagged in misery.

"Then, I help you finish it." Mirabella tried to sound confident.

"Easy to say," the ghost moaned. "But how are we going to figure out what it is, when we don't even know who I am?"

Mirabella watched helplessly as the apparition shivered and sobbed, bits of it floating away as if carried off on a winter wind, until it was completely gone.

Mirabella shivered. Being a ghost might not be much fun after all. If you really couldn't manipulate most solid items other than small ones. That would mean she'd never be able to take notes of her experiments. Worse, the idea of driving some innocent kid nuts just didn't seem right, much less amusing. To be the cause of such a horrible thing would be awful.

She had to find a way to help her friend.

CHAPTER TWENTY-THREE

Mirabella set the forks and knives on the table, placing them neatly beside the plates, with a half-folded napkin tucked under each knife. Her mother, puffy green oven mitts on both hands, removed a large pan of vegetable lasagna from the oven. Steam rose from the pan and filled the air with a tomato-saucy smell. Her mother had put a lot of extra cheese on the lasagna. She always complained it wasn't very healthy, but she loved the browned gooey mess almost as much as Mirabella did. Besides, she said that since there was no meat in it, a little extra cheese couldn't hurt.

Mirabella's mother set the lasagna on the cooling rack and turned the oven to broil. Mirabella's mouth watered as her mother popped the loaf of garlic bread under the broiler. The cold weather made her extra hungry and lasagna with garlic bread was one of her favorite meals.

"Mom?"

"What do you need, Mira?" Her mother was watching the

garlic bread through the window in the oven door, so it wouldn't burn. She'd been working a lot of extra hours and her eyelids drooped over her red-rimmed eyes.

"If you knew someone who needed help . . ." Mirabella pushed at a cuticle with her thumbnail. "What would you do?"

"I guess it depends."

"On what?"

"On several things." Her mother glanced at her, then turned back to the oven. "For example, is it the kind of help you can offer, or does this person need some kind of professional help?"

"I don't think it's the sort of thing for a professional."

"Is this person who needs help a friend or a stranger?"

Mirabella reached into the refrigerator for the milk. "Friend," she said after a moment. Not untrue. After all, the ghost had lived in the house longer than Mirabella and her mother. And it was certainly friendly toward her.

"But you don't really know them all that well, yet?" Her mother pulled the golden garlic bread out of the oven and slid it onto the wooden cutting board on the kitchen table. Garlic-scented steam wafted through the room.

"Not really." Mirabella finished pouring milk into two tall glasses and stuck the jug back in the refrigerator. Her mother brought the lasagna and the salad to the table.

"So, is this sort-of-a-friend in some kind of trouble?" she asked as they sat down to eat.

Mirabella scooped a huge helping of lasagna onto her plate. "It's more like needing help finding information."

"Research?" Her mother's face brightened with one of her I-think-I-see-where-this-is-going smiles.

Mirabella thought about it. "Yes."

"And that's something you're very good at, isn't it?"

Mirabella blushed. She didn't think her mother had ever

noticed all the things she researched and read about. Her father had. He had even encouraged her, often helping her track down resources and information on things like laser beams and mythological creatures. "I guess so." She chomped down on a crispy piece of garlic bread, the buttery flavor filling her mouth and the chopped garlic pieces tingling her tongue. That's probably all I need to do, she thought. Just a little research to help the ghost remember who it is. Or, rather, was.

Easy, right?

"I suppose you're going to be doing some research for someone then?" Her mother blew on a forkful of lasagna before taking a bite.

Mirabella nodded, her mouth too full of cheese and pasta to answer.

"Fine," her mother said. "Just don't let this extra research interfere with your school work."

"I won't." Mirabella mopped up some sauce with a piece of garlic bread and took a bite, chewing while she thought about where she should start. She glanced around the room, wondering if the ghost could see or hear them. "Do you know if any of the neighbors are the original owners of their houses?" she asked.

Her mother gave her an odd look, but continued to eat. "No. But I suppose your Aunt Clovinia would know if they were." She wore one of her how-did-we-end-up-talking-about-this looks. "You could always write to her and ask, if you really need to know." She studied Mirabella's face. "You know," she said finally, "helping a stranger is the sort of thing your father would do."

Mirabella crunched down on another piece of garlic bread. She didn't want to talk about her dad. Especially not with her mother.

"That was one of the things we had in common." Her

mother set down her fork and took a sip of milk.

What would her mother know about helping people? A surge of anger climbed up from Mirabella's chest and whooshed into her head. The garlic bread she'd been chewing tasted like burnt cardboard. It stuck in her throat when she tried to swallow. "If you had so much in common," she said in a rush. "Why did he have to leave? Why didn't you make him stay with us?"

Her mother's eyes flashed, then turned a dull brown. "You wouldn't understand, Mira," she said.

"Why do you always say that?" Mirabella shoved her plate away, knocking it into her half-empty glass and splashing milk across the table.

"Mira!" Her mother shoved her chair back and grabbed the kitchen towel from the oven door handle. "Get the sponge." Her mother mopped at the milk, trying to keep the spreading puddle from spilling over the edge and onto the floor.

Frozen in place, Mirabella sat and stared at the milky pool.

"Mira! What's wrong with you? Get the sponge and help me clean up this mess."

Mirabella rose to her feet in slow motion. A fire seemed to burn behind her eyes, but she had no tears to cool the heat.

CHAPTER TWENTY-FOUR

"That would be cheating," Mirabella said.

"I wouldn't call it cheating, exactly." Stacey twirled a lock of dark brown hair between her fingers. "You'd just be helping a friend with her homework."

"Helping would be working together, giving you suggestions or advice, or even looking over your paper before you turn it in. Not doing the assignment for you."

"You say hot, I say hawt! But it still means the same thing." Stacey shrugged.

"That's different, and not the same thing, at all," Mirabella said, shrugging her messenger bag strap into a new position. It weighed on her shoulder like a bag full of boulders. Outside, rain poured down, and the school hallway stank of wet tennis shoes and mud.

Stacey leaned close to Mirabella and hissed in her ear. "You wouldn't want your mom to find out you've been experimenting again, would you?"

"But I haven't—"

"Erin, did you hear what happened in Mrs. Flizzer's class today?" Stacey asked, batting her lashes innocently.

"You mean about her glasses disappearing?" Erin said, trying hard to keep a straight face and failing.

"Yeah," Stacey said. "I heard someone stole them right off her desk."

"Really? I wonder who would do an awful thing like that." Erin frowned.

"I don't know," Stacey said. "But I hope it wasn't some sort of trick. Or ex-per-i-ment." She drew out the last word, sounding out each syllable for emphasis.

A pounding grew inside Mirabella's head. It felt as if her heart had moved to where her brain should be and thumped against her skull, trying to break out. She stared at Erin and Stacey, but they were only dark shadows, outlines of people. They looked like the ghost had when it had first appeared, formless. Only instead of light and airy, they were dark, heavy blotches standing out against the grey metal lockers that lined the hallway.

"That's the sort of thing that could get someone into a lot of trouble, isn't it?" Erin said. "That is, if it really happened."

"It sure is." Stacey's lips curled up in a silky smile.

"Why would you do that?" Mirabella asked. "I thought we were friends."

"That's what you get for thinking," Stacey said. "Why would anyone actually want to be friends with you?"

Mirabella's shoulders slumped and her bag slid down her arm. "But we shared secrets!"

"You shared secrets," Stacey said. "We just told you stuff."

"But the cut on your leg." Mirabella pointed at Erin's shin.

Erin looked down at the floor. "Actually, my mom already knew all about it when I told you."

Mirabella turned to Stacey. "And that boy you kissed and stuff? Your parents don't actually know about that, do they?"

"You really don't know anything, do you?" Stacey shook her head. "I made that stuff up. Derek Sanders is the star of my mom's favorite soap, *Time Flies*."

Tears formed in Mirabella's eyes, and she willed herself not to let them fall. But one plump drop after another forced itself down her face. Erin's eyes widened and she started to say something, but Stacey cut her off.

"Hey, don't be such a big baby about it." Stacey smirked. "Here." She held out a brightly colored Hello Kitty folder. "When you finish the report, put it in here."

"But that's not fair!" Mirabella's voice was a hoarse whisper. It was all she could do to keep herself from wailing out loud. But she didn't want any of the other kids in the hallway to see her crying.

"It's not fair that we have to go to the same school as losers like you," Stacey said. "But that's the way it is." She shoved the folder at Mirabella. "Now take it. And make sure you do a good job."

Erin shifted from one foot to the other and glanced over her shoulder nervously. "Not too good a job," she said.

"Yeah." Stacey pursed her lips in thought. "Better just make it a B or a maybe a B plus. We don't want Mr. Pattison to get suspicious."

"But what about Mrs. Flizzer's glasses?"

"Funny thing about that," Stacey said. "Mrs. Flizzer's glasses turned up on her desk during recess. But they could disappear again. Just like that." She snapped her fingers in Mirabella's face. "You just do what we tell you to, and you won't have to worry."

Mirabella clutched the bright-colored folder in her fist and stared after the two girls as they sauntered down the hallway toward the exit doors. Tears stung her cheeks, but no one paid any attention to her.

She was invisible.

Again.

CHAPTER TWENTY-FIVE

"What are you doing?" the ghost asked.

"Sneezing and blowing my nose. Endlessly." Mirabella wadded up the tissue and tossed it into the wastebasket.

"Why?"

"Because I have allergies and this old house is full of dust," she grumped.

"Allergies?" The ghost drifted nearer.

Cold tendrils tickled Mirabella's face, like tattered fog wisping against her skin.

The ghost swayed a few inches in front of her. "I remember a time when . . ."

"Achoo!!" Mirabella slapped a tissue in front of her face, but it was too late.

The ghost's white form exploded in a swirl of tiny clouds that scattered around the room. Little puffs of pale gauze hovered in the air like suspended snowflakes. Mirabella's mouth dropped open. "I'm sorry!" she shouted, wondering if the poor ghost was all right.

In slow motion, the tiny puffs floated toward the middle of the room. One by one, they coagulated into a hazy blob. The blob rippled and became the ghost's fuzzy outline.

When it had reshaped itself, the ghost let out a soft sigh. "That felt very . . . odd." Its head tilted to one side. "Wait. I was remembering something. What was it?"

"I don't know," Mirabella said.

"I don't know either." The phantom floated across the room and settled on the bed like a sigh. Not really on the bed, more like in the bed, where it sank down until only its top half showed above the mattress. Mira was tempted to look under the bed to see if the ghost's feet stuck out below the box springs, but she stayed where she was. Instead she asked, "Doesn't that feel weird or painful?"

"What?" The ghost peered around uncertainly.

"Being in the bed like that." Mira pointed at the mattress.

"Oh!" The ghost seemed startled. "I hadn't noticed."

"Then I guess it must not."

"Must not what?"

"Hurt," Mira said.

The gauzy figure floated away from the bed. "The only pain I still feel," it whispered, "is not knowing who I am, or why I'm here."

The ghost's sorrow curled cold tendrils around Mirabella and for a moment she couldn't think of anything to say, until a violent sneeze broke the strange spell. "Don't you remember anything?" She dabbed at her tender nose with a fresh tissue.

"Flowers." The ghost shimmered for a moment, and Mirabella thought it would disappear again, but it turned toward the window, staring out at some forgotten moment. "Roses. Tea roses, I think. And a young man."

"A man?" Mirabella bounded up off the bed, her

excitement too much to contain. "Do you remember his name?"

"His name?"

"Yes. Maybe he was someone important. If you could remember his name, I might be able to find out something about him. About you!" She hopped from one foot to the other behind the pale figure, barely noticing the way the ghost's transparency turned the sky outside a milky blue.

"I only remember the roses—yellow ones—and the way he smiled when he gave them to me."

"He gave you flowers? Then he must have been important."

"Yes. I believe he was." The diaphanous form grew more distinct and the pale blue of the sky nearly disappeared behind it.

For an instant, Mirabella could make out the figure of a young woman in a long full skirt. "Try to remember his name," she encouraged.

The ghost's facial features contorted. Then it faded back to its usual blobby form, flickered, and blinked out like a burned out light bulb.

Frustrated, Mirabella sat down on the floor with a thump. How was she supposed to solve this mystery without the ghost's cooperation? She'd almost figured it out, almost come to know something of the person the ghost had been. Almost. But it seemed like every time they were on the verge of a discovery, the ghost disappeared. Like it didn't really want to remember.

Was that possible? Could the ghost be all sad and lonely and complain about having forgotten everything, but not really want to remember? Mirabella pulled her knees up and wrapped her arms around them. People said things all the time they didn't really mean. Like wedding vows and promising to always love each other and stay together, but then deciding not to. Or leaving and calling it a temporary separation.

She put her chin on her knees and stared out the window at the sky, wishing it was dark so she could see the stars.

CHAPTER TWENTY-SIX

Mirabella dropped her school bag on the floor and rummaged in the cupboard for some cookies. Her mother sat at the kitchen table, staring at a piece of paper, lips turned down in a thoughtful frown.

Mirabella poured herself a glass of milk and sat at the table. "What's that?" she asked between mouthfuls of vanilla wafers.

Her mother raised her eyes from the paper. "A letter. From Aunt Clovinia. She's finally had an offer. She's selling the house."

Mirabella choked down the cookies she'd been chewing. "What? But she can't."

"It's her house, Mira." Her mother folded up the letter.

Panic rose in Mirabella's throat. "But we practically just got moved in! Why would she sell it, now?"

"She says some developer is buying all the houses on the block. They're going to tear them all down and build some kind of townhouses or something. I guess they're offering her a lot of money. More than the house is worth."

"But, isn't there some way you could talk her out of it? At least for now? I mean, we'll have to move again and everything."

Her mother tapped the folded letter against the table. "We'll be fine. I've been able to save up some money so we can get an apartment somewhere."

"Mom, we can't move! Not now! Maybe not ever!"

"Living here was never meant to be permanent, Mira. You know that."

"But—"

"Besides, I thought you hated it here." Her mother wore her I-don't-really-understand-you-right-now look.

"I did." Mirabella dusted cookie crumbs from her hands and stared into her milk. "But now I need to . . ."

"You need to what?" Her mother wrinkled her forehead. "You're not doing some kind of experiment in this house, are you?"

"It's not an experiment." Mirabella scuffed her foot against the floor under the table.

"Then what, Mira? What is so important that you suddenly need to stay here in a house you have made it clear you hate?"

Mirabella tensed. Her mother was staring at her, her forehead wrinkled into an unhappy frown. Mirabella knew that look. Her mom was waiting for her to say the wrong thing. She couldn't tell her about the ghost, about what would happen to it when the house was torn down. How, if they left now, the ghost would be lost forever. There was no possible way her mother would believe her.

"Nothing." She shrugged. "It's nothing." *Nothing at all, Mom. I just have to save a ghost from becoming extinct. And now I have to do it before we get kicked out of this house.*

100

CHAPTER TWENTY-SEVEN

"I wish I could find some way to help you." Mirabella flopped down on her sproingy bed and propped her chin in her hands.

The ghost let out a wheezy sigh. "I'm afraid it's too late for me."

"No. Please, don't say that." Mirabella sat up. Her heart banged inside her chest so hard she thought she might break open.

"I've forgotten. All of it. Everything." The ghost drifted across the room and stared out the window at the specks of falling snow that fluttered silently past. "I tried to hold on, to remember. It seemed so important once. But now . . ." Its voice was heavy with sorrow.

"But you remember school! Jumping jacks! And—"

"And what?" The ghost slid across the room, trailing mist behind it, and hovered limply in front of Mirabella.

They couldn't give up, now. They just couldn't. "The

man," Mirabella said. "The one with the flowers. You said he was important." Her voice cracked.

The ghost sank down, its shape shifting into a sitting position, billows of white pillowing around it on the floor, like the skirt of a long white dress. It reminded Mirabella of one of her mother's wedding photos. The one of her sitting on the stairs with the train of her wedding gown spread out around her.

"Was he your husband?" she asked suddenly.

"He was supposed to be," the ghost sighed.

"You mean he was your fiancé?" Mirabella smacked her forehead with one hand.

"What?"

"The man," Mirabella nearly shouted. "He was supposed to be your husband, so you must have been engaged. Right?"

"I suppose so," the ghost's words were uncertain, but giddiness surged up inside Mirabella. She danced around the room. "You haven't forgotten everything! There's still hope."

The ghost rose from the floor and turned, watching Mirabella spin around and around.

Mirabella stopped dancing, took a running start and skated across the floor on the small throw rug. "We just have to figure out who you were going to marry."

"But how will we do that?" The ghost's voice trembled with fear and excitement. "I can't even remember who I am."

"Research." Mirabella jotted notes in her journal. "First, I'll find out about the house. There must be some information somewhere about when it was built and who lived in it. Maybe your family lived here. Or maybe . . ." Mirabella stopped. She'd been thinking out loud as she wrote and realized she didn't want to tell the ghost what had popped into her head. That maybe it was the spirit of someone who had died in the house. Died horribly. She shivered.

"Yes?" The ghost hovered over her.

"What?" Mirabella scribbled out the word "tragedy" with heavy lines to make it unreadable.

"You were saying something about my family. Although, I don't actually remember having a family. Of course, that doesn't mean much, does it? After all, I don't even remember my own name."

Mirabella continued to write, making sure not to put down anything that might upset the ghost. It had promised not to read her journal, but with everything else it had forgotten, it might easily forget that, too. And more than anything, Mirabella wanted to help it remember without causing it any more pain.

CHAPTER TWENTY-EIGHT

Mirabella wished she had a computer. It would make all this research so much easier. Her mother had been trying to save up to buy them one for a while, but there always seemed to be something that came up. The car would need fixing or the washing machine would break down.

Then again, maybe it was better that she'd had to come to the city courthouse. What if the ghost was the spirit of some poor murder victim and saw the information displayed on the monitor? Or someone who had been burned in a fire, or suffered some other terrible death? The poor thing was always so emotional, Mirabella would have to find a way to break the news gently. Besides, it turned out that most of the stuff she needed wasn't even accessible on a computer.

She loaded in the next film cartridge and turned the dial on the microfiche machine. How did people ever get anything done before computers? The Robertsville city records were in the process of being scanned into electronic files, but so far they'd only finished transferring as far back as 1980. All the older documents were kept on old-fashioned microfiche machines. The kind you had to load a film cartridge into and then turn the dial to scroll though the pages, one at a time, and then read through each page to find what you needed. There was no find or keyword search function.

She'd found out from the records clerk that the house on Rose Lane, along with all the others in that part of town, had been built in the late 1940s, but that was all the woman had been able tell her. The clerk, a short woman with curly gray hair, had helped Mirabella select the rolls of film—a huge pile of them—and then showed her how to use the microfiche machine. Then she went back to the front desk, leaving Mirabella alone to search the old records for 203 Rose Lane, through all the county building permits, one month at a time, starting with January 1945.

Mirabella's eyes watered and she dabbed at them with a tissue. The room smelled of wood polish and dusty old paper, and a flurry of sneezes caused her to bump the machine out of focus. Ugh! She must be allergic to the entire town. She blew her nose and readjusted her glasses.

Turning the knob brought the next page into view, but she had to adjust the focus in order to read the tiny words. Plot #495687, 203 Rose Lane. She sat bolt upright in the chair in excitement. This was it! The house on Rose Lane had been built in 1947. Mirabella almost leaped out of her seat, but then her jaw dropped in dismay. The building permit had been issued to MacDonald Construction. Her quest wasn't over, yet.

She wrote the name of the company in her journal, pulled the film from the machine and turned it off. Gathering up the spools of microfiche, she headed back to the clerk's desk.

"Did you find what you were looking for?" The gray-haired woman took the tray of film spools from Mirabella and checked them off her list.

"Sort of," Mirabella said, wrinkling her forehead. "I found the permit for the house, but it was built by a construction company, not a person like I thought it would be."

"That only makes sense." The clerk flashed Mirabella a bright smile. "Folks in town wouldn't have built their own houses much by then. They would have hired a contractor." She placed the film spools into a bin marked "Filing." "And folks outside of town wouldn't have bothered with a permit. So, you're lucky you were looking for a place inside the town limits."

"But how do I find out who owned the house?" Mirabella asked.

"You should have told me that's what you were looking for. You'll need to check with the County Recorder to get that information. What year did you say?"

"1947."

"Oh, dear." The clerk frowned. "I'm afraid that's going to be a problem."

"It is?"

"Yes. Sadly, those records were lost in a fire when the old courthouse burned down back in 1956."

Mirabella sagged against the counter. All of her research had gotten her exactly nowhere.

CHAPTER TWENTY-NINE

Mirabella sat on the park bench and stared at her notes. She shivered in the cold and her breath came out in ragged puffs of white, but she didn't want to go home and face the ghost just yet. She huddled over her journal. There must be some way to discover the history of the house. Granted, it wasn't a historical landmark. But Robertsville wasn't a huge city. Someone in town must know something about the 1940s.

That was it! If she could just find someone who knew the town's history, that person might be able to tell her about the house. Or give her some idea of where else to look. She leaped from the bench and stamped her feet to warm them up, then headed for the public library. Libraries had all sorts of historical stuff in them. She jogged across the town square and up the side street that led to the library. Huffing out clouds of vapor, she rushed up the marble steps two at a time and heaved open the door.

The front desk sat empty, the librarian, Mrs. Grant, was

nowhere in sight. Mirabella stood panting, catching her breath and gazing around at the tall shelves filled with row upon row of books. She still loved the sight of all those books. Fat ones, thin ones, short ones, tall ones. From beautiful art books to thick paperbacks, books were the friends you could count on. Characters in books were always there for you, anytime you revisited them by rereading their stories. They didn't change, or go away. They were yours for keeps.

The librarian came out of the stacks and Mirabella scooted across the room to the big oak desk. "Excuse me, Mrs. Grant," she said in a hushed voice.

"Hello again, Miss Polidoro. What may I help you with, today?" Mrs. Grant was a tall woman with a narrow pointy nose. Her bright red hair was pulled back from her face and held in place by two large butterfly clips. She looked about the same age as Mirabella's mother, but she had on a long flowing skirt and soft black boots.

Mirabella clutched her notebook. "I was wondering," she said, "if you might know where I could find some books on the history of Robertsville."

The librarian wrinkled her forehead and ran her finger down her thin nose. "I suppose it depends on what you're looking for," she said. "But if I were you, I'd check with the Robertsville Historical Society. They can tell you just about anything and everything about this town."

"I didn't know there was a Robertsville Historical Society," Mirabella said, trying to contain her excitement. "Where can I find them?"

"They don't actually have a location, and the membership roster isn't very extensive these days." Mrs. Grant sat down behind the desk and began typing something on her computer keyboard. "Several of their members died last year. They're mostly old-timers. But they still meet once a month." She continued tapping away at the keys. "Here we are." She turned the monitor so Mirabella could see it.

A website, filled with old-looking brown and yellow photos, covered the screen. Mirabella recognized the library building in one of the pictures. Across the top of the page was a banner that read: Robertsville We Grow Together.

"This is virtually the only place they're located." The librarian giggled at her own joke. Then shushed herself, even though there was no one nearby who could have been disturbed by her quiet laughter. "Here." She took out a scrap of paper and wrote out the webpage address and handed it to Mirabella. "You know where the public computers are?"

Mirabella nodded.

"Perhaps you can find what you need on the site." Mrs. Grant gave her a quick smile, then turned back to her work.

"Thank you." Mirabella took the slip of paper and retreated to the east room where a row of computers lined one wall. A bench sat off to one side and a sign on the wall read: Please limit your time to 60 minutes when others are waiting. The sign nearly made Mirabella laugh. Of the five computers, only the one on the far left was in use. Most people probably had computers at home these days.

She sat down in the first open seat and moved the mouse to wake-up the computer. The Robertsville Public Library main page popped up on the screen. Mirabella typed in the Web address for the Robertsville Historical Society, and took out her journal and a pen. Now she would find some answers.

After a while, the woman who'd been sitting at the computer on the far end, stood up. She glanced at Mirabella and gave her a friendly nod as she pulled her thumb drive from the computer's USB port and dropped it into her bag before hurrying out of the room.

Mirabella stretched and looked at the time on the computer.

Nearly two hours had passed. It was almost five o'clock and the library would be closing soon. She'd read page after page about the founding of Robertsville. How it began in 1842 as a small village with a general merchandise store that supplied a growing population of pioneers. How the first general store was opened in 1845. How the railroad had come through in 1855.

All the information she'd read was the kind of stuff her mother would have called colorful, and some of it was sort of interesting, but Mirabella was no closer to finding what she needed. She clicked back to the Robertsville Historical Society home page and stared at the list of Historical Society members. Most of the names on the list had tiny crosses next to them, which according to the small print at the bottom of the list marked the members who had died.

Only five names had no crosses next to them. One by one, Mirabella copied them down in her journal. If she went through the phonebook, maybe she could find a number for one of them and they might talk to her. She could always say it was for a school project. Adults would usually talk to you if you were doing a project for school. She bit her lip, thinking about the lie. She told herself it was only a little lie, and for a good cause, but the idea still bothered her. Maybe she could just say she was doing research and they wouldn't ask her what it was for. Maybe.

Mirabella was just about to copy the last name into her notebook when the lights flickered off and on again. Closing time. She moved the mouse to highlight the name so she could read it more easily and froze.

Mr. John Klutter.

She blinked and checked to see if she'd read the name correctly. Yep. John Klutter. Could it be—? The lights flicked off and didn't come back on. Mirabella had no more time to wonder about the name, she was too busy grabbing her coat and rushing toward the exit.

CHAPTER THIRTY

Mirabella stayed in her seat after the buzzer, pretending to organize her notes while the classroom emptied. She really needed to talk to Mr. Klutter about the Historical Society, but it seemed like every kid in class had questions about the Global Studies chapter they were working on. Who knew that history could be so confusing? But it was. Like the way Napoleon Bonaparte ended up in prison and yet became one of the most powerful men in the world, named himself emperor, then got exiled, escaped from exile to rule in France again, and then got exiled all over again. Mirabella shook her head. The whole thing sounded like a huge, messed up psychological experiment.

The only kids who didn't seem to have any questions about it were Erin and Stacey. In fact, Stacey hardly paid attention in class at all anymore, and Mirabella wondered how she planned to pass the test at the end of the section. How could she possibly expect to know the material when Mirabella was doing all her homework?

All at once, Mirabella's mouth went dry and her stomach got queasy. No, no, no, no, no! She could hardly even think about it. It was bad enough to do someone else's homework, but cheating on a test could get her into a load of trouble. And it was totally wrong! She put her head down on her desk and closed her eyes, trying to think about something else.

She was so upset she didn't notice that Mr. Klutter had settled into the desk beside her until he cleared his throat. Mirabella jerked her head up and her pencil rolled off the desk.

When Mr. Klutter leaned over to pick it up, the desk he was sitting in wobbled and tilted, one end rising high into the air. Mr. Klutter's shoes slipped and slid on the floor as he struggled to regain his balance.

Mirabella's mouth fell open. She wanted to do something, but she could only watch in fascination as the strange battle between man and desk took place. The desk wavered, and rocked before slamming back down onto the floor.

Mr. Klutter propelled himself out of the desk and stared at it like it was alive. "What a ride! Maybe I should join the rodeo." He grinned.

When Mirabella didn't answer, he shrugged, picked up the pencil and handed it to her. "Do you have a question about the homework, Mirabella?"

"No, Mr. Klutter." She tucked the pencil into the outside pocket of her bag.

"Then, I suppose you must have some other good reason for hanging out in my classroom during lunch. I'm sure you didn't come for the floorshow, as entertaining as it was. What can I do for you?" He gave her an encouraging look.

What if it wasn't him? Mirabella pinched the tip of one fingernail between the fingers of her other hand, twisting it back and forth. It just had to be him. "Are you the Mr. Klutter on the Robertsville Historical Society members list?"

He wrinkled his brow. "Why do you ask?"

Mirabella twisted her fingers together. She didn't want to tell a lie, but she really wanted to help the ghost. Only, she couldn't tell Mr. Klutter that. "I'm doing research on the old house that my mom and I moved into. It belongs to my Aunt Clovinia right now, but she's only lived in it for about ten years, I think." Not the entire story, but at least it wasn't a lie.

"I see." Mr. Klutter nodded in approval. "Research is a valid expenditure of one's time. Unfortunately," he shook his head, "I am not the Mr. Klutter who is a member of the Historical Society."

Mirabella's face fell. "Oh." Now what would she do?

"Fortunately, for you," Mr. Klutter gave her a lopsided smile, "that Mr. Klutter is actually my father and I'm sure he would be happy to answer a few questions about your house."

Mirabella's hopes rose like a balloon filled with helium.

"But . . ." Mr. Klutter held up a hand. "I can't guarantee he'll be able to tell you anything."

Mirabella's spirits dropped. She felt like a kid on a seesaw.

"Then again . . ." he held out his open hands, "he loves research as much or more than anyone I know. So, if he doesn't have the answers to your questions, he will undoubtedly find them. Why don't you write down your questions and give them to me. I'll ask him tonight and let you know something in the next couple of days."

"Thank you, Mr. Klutter. That'd be great!" Mirabella took out her notebook and wrote out her name and the address of the house in her best handwriting, so Mr. Klutter's father would have no trouble reading it. She chewed her thumbnail for a moment, then added several questions:

1. Who had the house built?

2. Who was the original owner?
3. Why did they sell the house?
4. Did something bad happen in the house?

She started to cross out the last question, but changed her mind. Then, she tore out the page and handed it to Mr. Klutter.

"I really appreciate this, Mr. Klutter."

"No problem at all." He took the paper from her. "It's the least I can do for a fellow researcher. Now, you'd better go eat before lunch hour is over."

Mirabella slung her messenger bag over one shoulder. "Thanks again." She hurried from the room, her feet gliding over the floor. She felt as light as the ghost must feel. That is, until she saw Stacey and Erin waiting for her in the hallway outside the classroom.

"What were you talking to Mr. Klutter about?" Stacey asked, her eyes slitting in suspicion.

"Nothing." Mirabella clutched at the strap of her school bag with nervous fingers.

"Then why did you wait for everyone else to leave before you talked to him?" Stacey pushed her finger into Mirabella's chest as she spoke.

Mirabella looked at Erin, but Erin stared wide-eyed at Stacey and said nothing. "I was just asking him about the Robertsville Historical Society, okay?" Mirabella's fingers twitched.

"The what?"

"The Robertsville Historical Society," Mirabella said more slowly.

"What's that?" Stacey frowned, her lips pushing outward.

"It's a group that studies the history of the town of Robertsville and then publishes the information on a website and stuff." Mirabella began to lose patience at Stacey's obvious ignorance, but the taller girl had a sharp edge to her that frightened Mirabella. It was like Stacey was a razor blade-covered bomb that might explode at any moment, and Mirabella didn't want to give her any reason to do that. She stopped and took a slow breath, the way her father had taught her, but her hands continued to worry at the strap. "I'm trying to find out about the history of my Aunt Clovinia's house," she said finally.

Stacey's mouth twisted into a snarl. "What for?" Her words were low and quiet, like she suspected Mirabella of lying.

"I . . ." Mirabella's mind raced. She adjusted her bag, shifting it to a more comfortable position. "I'm thinking about doing a report on it."

Stacey looked at her in suspicion. "Why?"

"For extra credit," Mirabella blurted.

"You need extra credit?" Stacey barked in disbelief.

"Sure," Mirabella lowered her voice and tried to look embarrassed. "I—I didn't do so well on the last test." She stared down at the frazzled toes of her shoes.

"Hah!" Stacey laughed and it turned into a snort. "Miss Smarty-brains didn't get a hundred percent on something and she's doing extra credit to make up for it." She turned to Erin, who was gaping at Mirabella in surprise. "That's so dumb."

Stacey spun around to face Mirabella. "That better be all you were talking to him about, or you know what will happen." She made circles with her fingers and held them in front of her eyes to make it look like she was wearing glasses.

The canvas strap on Mirabella's heavy bag seemed to cut into her shoulder like a sword blade. She knew exactly what Stacey meant. She would steal Mrs. Flizzer's glasses and then tell any adult who would listen that Mirabella had done it as an experiment. Then, when Mirabella's mother found out . . . Mirabella bit her lip to keep it from trembling. She couldn't risk getting in trouble. Not now.

Stacey dropped her hands and laughed. She grabbed Erin by the sleeve and pulled her down the hallway toward the lunchroom, cracking up and repeating the words "extra credit" in a loud voice.

There was a noise behind her and Mirabella turned to see Mr. Klutter standing in the doorway to his classroom. "Is everything all right?" he asked.

No, she thought, everything is not all right. Everything has been wrong ever since my mom moved us to this crummy town! Then she realized that everything, absolutely everything, had started to go wrong the day her parents sat her down and told her they would be living apart for a while.

Her throat closed up and she struggled to answer him. "They were just making sure I, um, knew it was pizza day."

Mr. Klutter's brow wrinkled. "Apparently, pizza is critically important to some people." His gaze swept down the hallway where Stacey and Erin had disappeared. "If you need any help, you know, with school work, or anything, you let me know. All right?"

"Sure, Mr. Klutter." Mirabella waved and started to back away down the hall. "I will." Sure, I will, she thought. Because that's just what I don't need is a teacher butting in. That would make Stacey real happy. She'd probably think up something extra horrible to blame on me. "Thanks again for asking your dad about the house. I really appreciate it."

"No problem," Mr. Klutter said.

She waved good-bye, spun around, and headed toward the lunchroom. She wished she could find a quiet place where she could hide. Someplace where no one would bother her, like the janitor's supply closet. But the door to the storeroom was always locked. She'd tried it more than once.

Her stomach churned and she knew she'd never be able to

eat her lunch. Between worrying about what Stacey and Erin might do and her inability to help the poor ghost, she didn't think she'd ever be able to eat again.

CHAPTER THIRTY-ONE

The clock by the bed seemed to have warped into another dimension, one where time stood still. Mirabella peered through the dark at the glowing numbers. Only five minutes later than the last time she'd checked. Should she tell her mom about Erin and Stacey? About the homework?

She rolled over and slugged her pillow and slammed her head into the dent she'd made in it. Thinking her mom would understand was as stupid an idea as believing that Erin had invited her over because she liked her and wanted to be friends. Her mom would just freak out and probably not listen to Mirabella long enough for her to explain things. She never really listened anymore.

She yawned and wiped at her eyes. Yawning always seemed to make them water. She sniffed and reached for a tissue, but her hand knocked the box off the nightstand and it landed on the floor with a muffled thud.

"What's wrong?" a voice hissed from the corner of the

room.

Mirabella bolted up in the bed and gripped the edge of the covers. "Is that you?" she gasped.

"If you mean me, whoever I am," the ghost replied, "the answer is yes."

Mirabella peered at the blurry figure perched in the old overstuffed chair. In the darkness, the ghost looked more solid. Without any light shining through it, it seemed more real, more like a regular person. "How long have you been sitting there?" Mirabella kept her voice low so her mother wouldn't hear.

"Since you turned out the light," the ghost whispered back.

"Do you sit there every night?" Mirabella knew she should be creeped out by the idea of someone sitting in the room watching her as she slept, but she wasn't. In fact, it was kind of comforting that the ghost seemed to be keeping watch over her. It was almost like having her own personal guardian angel.

The ghost was quiet for a long time. "Yes," it said, finally. "For some reason, it soothes me to watch you sleep." There was another pause. "Most nights you are very still. Only, tonight you haven't slept well, at all. Is there something wrong?"

Mirabella wondered if she could tell the ghost about Stacey and Erin. *There are these girls at school and they tricked me into telling them a secret about myself and now they're using it to make me do their homework*, she imagined herself saying. Her problem sounded so lame when she put it that way. Especially compared to being trapped in a broken down house without knowing why or even who you used to be.

Anyway, what would be the point? It wasn't like the ghost could do anything about it. She shook her head and shrugged, then wondered if the ghost could see her in the dim gray of the room. "I just have a lot on my mind."

Cold air drifted in under the covers and Mirabella hugged

the blankets for warmth. "I wish I knew what to call you," she said. "It just doesn't seem right to say 'you' all the time."

There was a soft sighing sound, like the brush of fabric against itself as the ghost floated across the room. It hovered in a ray of light that snuck in between the aging drapes, and glowed softly in the moonlight.

"There was a woman who came here a few times. She never stayed for long, but she called me by a name."

"A woman? But I thought you said no one ever saw you before me." Mirabella stacked her pillows up behind her so she could sit up and see the ghost better.

"She never saw me," the ghost said. "But she knew I was here."

"What did the woman look like?" Mirabella asked.

"She was short and thin. Her face was wise and her fingers were long and slender. She wore loops of beads and crystal earrings, and painted her fingernails bright colors. Colors I'd never seen on anyone's nails before. Mostly shades of purple."

"That must have been G'ma, I mean, my grandmother," Mirabella said. "My mother says she believed the house was— occupied, so she wouldn't sleep here. She lived in a house in the woods and used to see fairies and things, too. Only nobody believed her. Except me. Of course, I was really little, then. So, I guess it didn't count for much."

"I imagine it counted a great deal to her," the ghost said.

"So, what did she call you?" Mirabella asked, gulping down her sudden sadness. She missed her G'ma.

"I think she called me Ariel. Though I don't know why."

"I don't know either," Mirabella yawned. "But it's pretty."

"I suppose," the phantom said, "but I don't really feel like I belong to it." It sank down onto the edge of the bed. "Now, why don't you snuggle down and get some sleep?" The ghost began to hum a tune. Not a lullaby exactly, but something else calm and soothing.

Mirabella slid down under the covers and closed her eyes, listening to the rise and fall of the ghost's lilting voice.

CHAPTER THIRTY-TWO

"Mirabella, please see me after class." Mr. Klutter replaced the cap on the marker he'd been using to write the homework assignment on the whiteboard, and sat at his desk. His hands were smeared with blue splotches from using his fingers to erase the board.

The buzzer sounded, followed by the slamming of books and the garbled noise of twenty-five kids all talking at the same time. A couple of boys began to toss a baseball back and forth as they headed for the door, but one shake of Mr. Klutter's head made the ball disappear into a backpack.

Mirabella slid her books into her bag. Her fingers fluttered with nervous energy as she tucked her pencils into an inside pocket. It had been four whole days since Mr. Klutter agreed to give her list of questions to his father. She'd begun to think he'd forgotten. She suddenly froze in the midst of zipping her bag shut. What if this wasn't about the house? What if he knew about the homework? She peeked warily up at him, but he wasn't looking at her. He seemed to be searching his desk for something.

As soon as the other students had left the room, she approached Mr. Klutter's desk, trying not to look guilty.

"How're you doing, today?" Mr. Klutter asked while sifting through a stack of papers.

"Okay, thanks." Mirabella scuffed the toe of her shoe against the bottom of his desk.

He straightened another pile, making sure the papers all faced the same direction, with all the student's names in the upper right hand corners. "Good. And how are things going in the rest of your classes?" He scratched at his nose, smearing a streak of blue down the left side of it.

"Great." She tried to sound enthusiastic. Why was he asking a bunch of questions about her classes? She gulped back her fear, telling herself to stay calm, to wait and see.

He opened a drawer and closed it. "Sorry. I know I have it here somewhere."

Mirabella shifted her weight.

He rummaged through another drawer and pulled out a piece of lined yellow paper. "Here it is." There were notes on the paper, written in pencil. The writing was cramped, printed in tiny block letters, but Mirabella could make out a few words and a number—203. The address of the house on Rose Lane. Relief pushed aside fear and then excitement took over. Her body tensed, tingling with anticipation.

"I'm afraid my father doesn't know who built the house, but he remembered that the original owner never lived there. There was some sort of family tragedy or something."

Her stomach heaved. Oh, no. The poor ghost. Something bad *had* happened in the house.

"He says he knew the family that lived there, said they were good people. He went to school with one of their boys. I guess they owned a stationary store or something, back in the day, as he put it." Mr. Klutter laughed.

"Thanks, Mr. Klutter." She tried not to sound disappointed, but her voice cracked.

"I'm sorry." Mr. Klutter's face grew serious. "I wish I could have been more help. I guess this is pretty important?"

"Yeah." Mirabella inspected the paper again, wishing it held more than just another clue. "It's real important." She folded the paper into a neat square.

"Well, maybe you can track down the family that lived there. My father seemed to think they might still be in town. They should be able to tell you who they bought it from."

"That's a great idea." Mirabella forced herself to sound grateful. Of course, tracking down the name on the paper would be the logical next step. It wasn't like she hadn't already thought of it herself, but she was running out of time. She needed answers now, not another clue to chase. "Thanks, Mr. Klutter."

"No problem." He pulled his blue vinyl lunch bag out from under his desk. "Let me know if I can be of any further assistance to you."

Mirabella stuck the piece of paper in the back pocket of her jeans. "By the way," Mirabella said, "you have some of that dry erase marker on your nose."

Mr. Klutter focused down his nose, eyes crossing. "What do you know?" He grabbed a tissue from the box on his desk and wiped at the mark. "How's that?" He stuck his nose out for Mirabella to inspect.

There was still a light smudge of blue, like a faded bruise. "Better," she said.

"Thank you." He pulled out a bright red apple and polished it on the front of his shirt. "I wouldn't want to go around looking silly, or the other teachers might laugh at me." He grinned.

"You're welcome." Mirabella headed for the hallway, wondering if he meant it, or if he was just trying to be funny.

"Oh, and one more thing," Mr. Klutter called after her.

Mirabella froze. He did know about the homework! She'd been so careful to make sure the answers didn't match exactly, but . . . Her chest tightened, squeezing the breath inside her. Preparing for the worst, she donned her most innocent look and turned back toward him.

"Good luck on your quest." He raised the glossy apple in salute before taking a huge bite.

CHAPTER THIRTY-THREE

Mirabella took out the sheet of paper and unfolded it, then flipped open the thin phonebook she'd found in the pantry. She ran her finger down the list of names under "S," searching for William Smith, the person who, according to Mr. Klutter's father, had bought the house after it was built.

There were about a hundred Smiths in the book, but only two William Smiths and one Bill Smith. She drew a tiny star next to each name in red ink. She'd learned that Bill was a nickname for William when her class had studied the forty-second president of the United States, Bill Clinton.

She picked up the telephone and dialed the first number. There was a hollow ringing on the line, like the call had to go through a tunnel to get to the Smith's house.

The ringing continued and she chewed her bottom lip. What if none of the people in the phonebook was the William Smith she was looking for? What if he'd moved out of Robertsville? What if he was gone, like G'ma? Like her dad?

She shoved that thought down and instead tried to calculate how old Mr. Smith would be if he'd bought the house when it was new. He would have had to be at least old enough to have finished high school and have a job, so at least eighteen. Could you buy a house when you were only eighteen? Maybe he'd been older than that. If the house was built in 1947, that would make him at least eighty-something, which was pretty old. G'ma was only seventy-eight when she died, but lots of people lived to be older than that, didn't they? Unless they were in some kind of accident and didn't recover.

The phone kept ringing. Should she stay on the line and wait? How many rings would it take to answer if you were in your eighties? She twisted a curl of hair between her fingers, pulling it out to see how long it would be if it were straight. A sudden click made her jump and yank on her hair. A voice came on the line. She untangled her finger from the curl, and licked her lips.

"You have reached the Smith residence. Please leave a message at the beep and we'll get back to you just as soon as we may." The voice on the answering machine was a woman's. She had a British accent and she sounded too young, but Mirabella cleared her throat as the long beeeeeep sounded in her ear.

"Hi," she said. "Um, you don't know me, but I'm doing some, um, research and I'm looking for the William Smith who used to live at 203 Rose Lane. If you could please call me back, my name is Mirabella Polidoro and my number is 530-555-2612." She started to hang up, stopped and added, "Thank you."

She made a face and hung up. Lame. She'd sounded completely dumb, and whoever listened to the message would probably just erase it.

She pushed her bangs out of her eyes and punched in the

next number.

This time a man answered on the first ring. "Hello?"

"Hello." Mirabella said in her most polite voice. "I'm looking for Mr. William Smith."

"Whatever it is you're selling, I don't want any, and take me off your calling list," the man growled.

"I'm not actually selling anything." Mirabella told him. "I just—"

"Sure, you're not. You just want to give me a free weekend stay in the Bahamas. All I have to do is come down and spend my valuable time listening to some sales pitch."

"No, sir," Mirabella tried again. "I'm a student, and—"

"I don't need any magazines. I've got all the reading material I want."

"This isn't about magazines," Mirabella said. "It's about a house. On Rose Lane. I'm looking for the William Smith who used to live there." She hurried to get the words out before the man could cut her off again.

"Well, why didn't you say so? I've never lived on Rose Lane, so I'm not him and, before you ask, no, I don't know him." A resounding click told Mirabella the man had hung up on her.

Mirabella held out the receiver and stared at it. No wonder her mother said the last place she'd ever work was in telephone sales.

She rubbed at her nose, which tickled from her allergies, and stared at the last starred name on her list. Bill Smith. She wondered how likely it would be for a man in his eighties to have his name listed as Bill, instead of William. Weren't most adults that age kind of formal and proper? Well, except for G'ma of course. But G'ma had been the exception to the adult rule for most things. Even the younger adults seemed to think she was unusual. She'd even heard one of them say G'ma was funny, and not as in haha funny.

She picked up the phone and put it down again. She really didn't want to talk to anyone else like the man who'd just hung up on her. But how else was she going to find Mr. Smith? She reached for the handset, but before she could pick it up, it rang. She flinched, startled by the unexpected sound. She picked the phone up and hit the talk button. "Hello?"

"Good afternoon," a woman said, in a strong English accent. "I'm attempting to reach a Mirabella Polidoro."

"This is Mirabella."

"Very good. Well then. My name is Agnes Smith. You rang up earlier asking after my father-in-law, Mr. William Smith. Is that correct?"

"Yes," Mirabella nearly yelped.

"I believe you were seeking information regarding Mr. Smith's earlier residence. The house on Rose Lane?"

"Yes." Breathless, Mirabella held the receiver to her ear with both hands and her voice came out in an excited squeak. "Is Mr. Smith available? I'd really like to ask him some questions about the house."

"I am terribly sorry," Mrs. Smith said. "But I'm afraid Mr. Smith passed away last month."

"Oh," Mirabella said. Then, remembering the words she'd heard over and over at her father's funeral, she added, "I mean, I'm very sorry for your loss."

"Yes, thank you. It was especially difficult for my husband, you know. They were very close."

Mirabella's throat tightened. "I understand," she said, her heart collapsing as she realized she'd run into another wall. "And I'm sorry to have bothered you."

"No bother at all," Mrs. Smith said. "I've fielded a number of calls since William's passing. It's easier on my husband, you see." There was a pause and a distinct rustling of papers on the line.

"Thank you for calling me back, Mrs. Smith." Mirabella prepared to hang up.

"Right then. As to the business at hand," the woman continued. "I have some old papers here, quite a large stack actually, including the ownership papers from the house, I believe. I was planning on shredding them and tossing them into the dust bin, but I hadn't quite gotten 'round to it." There was more paper shuffling.

"Excuse me." Mirabella's grip tightened on the phone. "Did you say you had some papers from when Mr. Smith owned the house?"

"Yes. I'm certain they're here somewhere. Would you mind terribly holding the line while I look?"

"Yes. I mean, no, I don't mind holding."

"Right then. Just one moment."

Mirabella pressed the receiver closer to her ear, as if she would be able to hear when Mrs. Smith found what she was searching for. There was movement and a mumbling. It sounded like Mrs. Smith was talking to herself while sorting through a stack of papers. After what seemed like forever, there was a satisfied "aha," and Mrs. Smith came back on the line.

"I have it right here," she said, obviously pleased with herself. "Now, what was your question?"

"Did Mr. Smith own the house in 1947?" Mirabella tried to force herself to stay calm. She didn't want to get her hopes up, just to be let down again. But she gripped the handset in both hands as she waited for the response.

"Let me see. Yes. It appears he bought the house that very year."

Mirabella took a big gulp of air before asking her next question. "Do the papers say who he bought the house from?"

"Yes. The seller's name is a bit fuzzy, but it appears the

house was purchased from a Mr., no, I'm sorry, I believe it says Dr. Would you please hold the line another moment while I find my spectacles."

"Sure." Mirabella counted to ten. She stood up. She sat down. Then she counted to ten again.

"Where the devil did I put those reading glasses? Oh, here they are, right where I left them. I'm terribly sorry about that. That's much better. Right then. The seller's name was Dr. Richard Benniton."

Mirabella leaped up and danced around the room. That was it. The name she'd been looking for. The man who built the house was a Dr. Richard Benniton. "Thank you so much!" she squealed.

"I'm sure it was nothing. No trouble at all, my dear. I hope it helps with whatever project you're working on."

"Oh, yes!" Mirabella said. "It helps a lot. Thank you, so very much, Mrs. Smith. Thank you for calling. It was wonderful talking to you."

"Lovely to chat with you as well, my dear. Good-bye now. And all the best."

"Good-bye. And thanks again." Mirabella hung up and twirled around in a circle until she got so dizzy she flopped onto the floor in a happy heap.

CHAPTER THIRTY-FOUR

Mirabella searched the yellow pages, the medical listing, and even the white pages. Unfortunately, she hadn't asked Mrs. Smith to spell the name for her, so she tried spelling it every way she could think of, but she could find no Dr. Benniton. There was a chance that Dr. Benniton was a dentist, or even a professor, so she checked every possibility. Still no luck. There weren't any Bennitons listed in the entire Robertsville directory. She leaned back against her bed, and chewed her thumbnail.

A cold breeze wafted across her shoulders and she shut the phonebook, slapping the pages together in a rush.

"What's that you're doing?" The ghost hovered over her shoulder, eyeing the book.

Should she tell the ghost that she'd tracked down the name of the original owner of the house? She recalled the roller coaster feeling of having her hopes raised and dashed again. Mirabella still hadn't actually found the person. What if she never did?

"I was just looking for a doctor." Mirabella pushed the phonebook away and closed her notebook, even though she no longer wrote detailed notes in her journal, since she didn't want the ghost to see them before she was ready to share what she'd discovered.

"You aren't ill, are you?" The ghost sounded worried. It reached a hand toward Mirabella's forehead in a motherly gesture, but stopped short and the pale hand fell away.

"No." Mirabella assured it. "It's nothing like that."

"Another school project, then?"

"Sure," Mirabella said without thinking, then cringed inside at how easy it was becoming to lie.

The ghost floated toward the chair in the corner of the room. "Perhaps, I can help."

Mirabella sprang up. "It's not actually an assignment," she said, grabbing her books. "It's just something I was sort of thinking about."

"Are you going somewhere?" The ghost drooped.

Mirabella froze. She couldn't tell the ghost the truth, not yet, and she couldn't tell her friend another lie. "I have to go to the library," she said. "And I thought I'd maybe look up doctors." At least that was true.

"You should ask your mother," the ghost murmured.

"It's Saturday, and it's just the library," Mirabella snapped. "I don't have to ask her about every little thing." She shoved her notebook into the outside pocket of her bag.

"I meant about doctors," the ghost whispered so low Mirabella almost missed it. "She is a nurse, isn't she?"

"Oh, yeah. Right." Mirabella bit her lip. "Sorry. I thought you meant I had to ask her permission just to leave the house and go a few blocks to the library."

"I know what you thought," the ghost replied. "Although,

I'm not sure I understand why the suggestion should make you so angry."

Mirabella collapsed onto the bed. Why *did* the idea of having to ask her mother's permission to go somewhere make her so angry? She dug at her fingernails. She had no answer. She just knew that having to ask her mother's permission to do anything lately felt like asking the prison warden for more bread and water.

The ghost waited, sitting up so straight and patient it reminded Mirabella of how Mr. Klutter sat at his desk when he was waiting for one of the students to answer a question he had asked.

"That's actually not a bad idea," she mumbled.

The ghost leaned forward, putting a faint hand to where its ear would be, if it had ears. "Pardon me?"

"I said, it's not a bad idea. You know. Asking my mom about the doctor, I mean, doctors." Mirabella slipped on her shoes, then slid the strap of her messenger bag over her shoulder and stood up. "I'll, um, I'll see you later," she told the ghost.

"I expect so." The milky figure dissolved until the chair sat empty. The words, "Be safe" whispered through the room.

Mirabella eyed the empty chair. Why did the idea of asking her mother how to find Dr. Benniton make her squirm? It made perfect sense that nurses and doctors in a town the size of Robertsville would know one another. So, her mother would probably know who to ask, at least. Only, what if her mother asked her why she was looking for Dr. Benniton. What would she say? What could she say? She shrugged. She'd think of something on the way.

By the time she reached Dr. Worth's clinic, she still hadn't thought of a good excuse other than the old standby of research for a school project. It usually did the trick, but in this case it sounded lame, even to Mirabella. After all, what kind of school project would require her to find some old retired doctor that most likely no one in town had even heard of?

When Mirabella entered the waiting room, she found the clinic's receptionist, Antonia, feeding the fish. Mirabella sidled up to watch the bright saltwater fish swirl around the huge lump of coral that rose like a fairy castle in the middle of the tank. Antonia turned and smiled brightly at her.

"Hola, Mirabella. ¿Cómo estas?"

"Muy bien, gracias ¿y tú?" Mirabella answered, using up half her Spanish vocabulary.

"Igualmente," Antonia said. "¿Quieres hablar con tu mamá?"

"Um, sí. I think," Mirabella said. "If that means, do I want to talk to my mom."

"Sí." Antonia nodded her head. "Muy bien, muchacha! Very good. You will be speaking Spanish in no time."

Mirabella grinned. She hardly knew any Spanish words, and she liked that Antonia taught her new ones whenever she visited the clinic. "Is my mom busy?"

"She is assisting the doctor with a patient, but you can wait for her. It should not be too much longer. Or I can take a note to her, if you prefer."

Mirabella leaned on the counter and looked through the window toward the back where a wide hallway led to the examining rooms. On one side of the hall there was a drinking fountain and a scale where her mother would weigh the patients before taking them into a room to wait for the doctor.

She shifted her weight back and forth, nervous energy zinging around inside her. She still hadn't figured out what to tell her mother about why she was looking for some doctor she'd never met. She hoped she'd think of something while she waited. "I just want to ask if she might know how I can find

136

someone who used to be a doctor here."

"In this office?"

Mirabella thought for a moment. "I don't really know," she said. "All I have is his name, Dr. Richard Benniton."

The receptionist's face lit up. "Oh, sí, I know the doctor. I worked for him when I first graduated from school," she said. "He was a very nice man, but sad all the time. His practice was on the other side of the street from the bank." She tapped her chin with one finger. "But he retired some time ago. I believe he moved to Loring's some few years back."

"You mean the place where all the old people live?" Mirabella asked.

"Sí, niña, pero I believe they prefer to be called senior citizens, eh?"

"Oh. Sorry. Do you know if he's still there now?"

"Yo no se," Antonia said. "But it could be."

"Thank you. I mean, muchas gracias, Antonia."

"No problema, mija."

Mirabella headed for the door.

"You don't want to see your mamá?" Antonia asked.

Mirabella looked at the clock. Part of her was dying to finally talk to Dr. Benniton, the rest of her was wondering how she was going to get three sets of homework done tonight. It was already almost five o'clock. "That's okay, Antonia. I have a lot of homework. I'll talk to her when she gets home."

CHAPTER THIRTY-FIVE

"So where's my homework?" Stacey held out her hand.

Mirabella cringed. With the phone calls and chores and her own homework last night, she hadn't had time to do both Stacey and Erin's homework, too. "I'm really sorry," she said.

"I'm really sorry," Stacey mimicked. "Erin, do you know what I think? I think Marbles doesn't want to be friends anymore." She made the shape of glasses with her hands and shook her head. "That's too bad."

"But, I—"

"It's your choice," Stacey continued. "It really could have been a great relationship. But if you want to break up the band, we can't really stop you, I suppose." Stacey made her voice wistful and sad, but she wore an ugly sneer.

"I have part of it done. One extra copy, anyway." Mirabella held out the homework to Stacey like a peace offering.

Stacey frowned. "But that's not what we agreed. Is it, Erin?"

Erin watched Stacey the way a wounded bird might watch a hungry predator.

Stacey turned on Erin. "I said, that's not what we agreed. Right, Erin?" She jabbed Erin in the ribs with her elbow. A yelp escaped Erin's lips and she nodded her head.

"I can't hear you," Stacey said, her voice a low growl.

"Yes. No. I mean, right." Erin gabbled, her head bobbing up and down.

Mirabella had thought the two girls were friends, that they bullied her together because they were a team. But now Mirabella thought she saw fear in Erin's eyes. She wondered what it was that Stacey knew about Erin that made her do whatever she wanted, including helping her to pick on other girls.

Stacey snatched the paper away from Mirabella. "Now, give me yours."

"Mine?" Mirabella backed away.

"Yes, yours." Stacey closed on her. "You owe us two sets of homework, and you've only handed over one. So. Give. Me. Yours." Stacey's mouth twisted in anger. "And it had better be done in pencil, so we can erase your name."

She reminded Mirabella of an angry wildcat. Mirabella looked at Erin, but Erin averted her eyes. Mirabella reached into her bag and fumbled with her homework.

Stacey grabbed the paper, practically tearing it in two. "That's better," she said, handing the paper to Erin who took it between two fingers as if she were picking up a nasty piece of garbage. "You'll probably want to wrinkle it up, too," Stacey told the other girl. "Just to make sure the teacher doesn't recognize the super neatness."

Erin held the paper at arm's length.

"Put it away," Stacey commanded. "Before someone sees it."

Without looking at Mirabella, Erin slid the paper into her binder.

"Now." Stacey said. "Let's make sure this doesn't happen again." She turned to leave, but stopped, a half smile crawling across her face. "Oh, and there's a test coming up in Math class. You better figure out how we're going to get at least an 89%. Each. In fact, make mine a 90%. It's time I brought my grades up." She turned on her heel and marched away.

Erin stared at Mirabella for a moment. She opened her mouth to say something, but Stacey hissed at her over her shoulder and Erin hurried to catch up.

Stunned, Mirabella stood in the hallway, staring after them. She should have said no. She should have done something. Anything. Instead, she had simply handed over her homework, just because Stacey had told her to. She had been a total wimp. She didn't have today's homework to turn in. And now, nightmare come true, Stacey wanted her to cheat on a test.

Mirabella had never cheated on anything! She couldn't even seriously think about cheating without her whole body growing cold and jittery. And if her mother found out, she'd be grounded for a bazillion years. Even though none of this would have ever happened if her mother hadn't decided to move them to this stupid town!

CHAPTER THIRTY-SIX

"Dr. Benniton," the nurse called, rapping on the door.

"What is it, Roger?" a gravelly voice responded.

The nurse pushed the door open a few inches and stuck his head into the room. "You have a visitor, Dr. Benniton."

"I do? Who is it?"

"A young girl. Says her name is Mirabella Polidoro. I think she's doing a report on the history of Robertsville. She says she'd like to ask you a question or two."

"Help me into my chair, will you, Roger? I'm feeling a bit tired."

"Perhaps, you should rest, then," the nurse said. "I can ask her to come back some other time."

"Nonsense," the older man said. "It isn't like I get visitors every day. Just help me into my chair. I'll be fine."

"Sure, Dr. Benniton." The nurse disappeared into the room.

Mirabella stood in the hall and waited, silently thanking Antonia. Finally, she had tracked down the man who had built the house. The man she was sure must hold the key to the identity of the forgetful ghost. The school day had lasted forever, each class taking an eternity, and anticipation building with every moment. But now she was finally here at Loring's, standing outside the room of the man who could have the answers she'd been seeking for so long. The answers that could help free the ghost from imprisonment.

The door to Dr. Benniton's room swung open and Roger stepped out.

"Come in, come in. No need to dawdle out there." A very old man sat hunched in a black and silver wheelchair with a blanket covering his legs. He waved a gnarled hand, gesturing for her to enter.

Mirabella hesitated. Her throat went suddenly scratchy and her fingers twitched. What if it isn't him? she thought.

"It's okay." Roger smiled. "His growl is worse than his bite."

The old man raised an eyebrow.

"And," Roger continued, "a little company will be good for him."

Squaring her shoulders, Mirabella walked into the room, crossing her fingers for luck.

She had expected Loring's to be more like a hospital. It had the same disinfectant smell, the same plain white hallways. Only, Dr. Benniton's room looked like a room in someone's house. The bed was a hospital bed, and the wheelchair Dr. Benniton sat in was a regular wheelchair, but there was also a couch with small tables at each end, and none of the beeping machines she'd pictured. She relaxed a little and her messenger bag slid down her arm.

"Sit. Sit." Dr. Benniton waved her toward the couch with a shaky hand. His weathered and wrinkled face resembled the skin of a raisin. His blue eyes were faded and his hair, what little there was, wisped about his head like a fine layer of cotton candy.

Mirabella sat down and pulled out a notepad and a pen. "Is it all right if I take some notes?" she asked.

"Aha. You're a journalist, then?" Dr. Benniton leaned back with a small groan. "Fine. Fine. Now, what can I tell you about, eh? The big flood? The history of the town's founder? There's even a little scandal in that story." He waggled his eyebrows.

Mirabella shook her head. "Thank you, no," she said. "I'm actually more interested in the house on Rose Lane."

He stiffened. "Sadie's house," he said, his voice thick and raspy.

Mirabella leaned forward. "Sadie?"

CHAPTER THIRTY- SEVEN

"We were to be married in March." Dr. Benniton's shoulders hunched and his hand jerked about stiffly on the end of his bony arm. The framed picture he held shivered in his shaky grasp. "This was my Sadie." He handed it to Mirabella.

The faded photograph was tinged brown, its edges worn from being handled. A young woman gazed out, her dark hair flipped under at her chin. She wore high heels, a long flared skirt that fell just above the ankles, and a fitted jacket. A flat round hat tilted off the side of her head so far it must have been pinned in place to keep it from sliding off. She held a bouquet of flowers, and instead of looking directly at the camera, her head was turned a little to the left and she wore a wide smile, happy, shy, and dazzling all at once.

"What was she looking at?" Mirabella asked.

"Not what. Who." Mr. Benniton's eyes sparkled. "Me. She was looking at me. I'll always remember the way she looked at me that day." He sighed, and his breath wheezed out. "We were in love," he whispered.

Mirabella handed the photo back to him and he stared at it in silence. After what seemed like forever, his sorrowful eyes met hers. "We were going to live in that house, she and I and our many, many children. We made so many plans."

"What happened?" Mirabella asked.

"Life," he said. "Which, back then, often meant death. We didn't have the kinds of advanced medicine and technology we have now, you know. The simplest thing could lay a body low. And in my Sadie's case, she never got up again."

"She got sick? With some horrible disease?"

"Yes," he said. "Polio. A very horrible disease."

"But isn't there a vaccine for polio?" Mirabella thought she remembered her mother mentioning it when they'd talked about the vaccines they gave babies at the clinic.

"Not then. Not in 1947. Not until Dr. Salk came up with one a few years later. Just a few years. But my sweet Sadie was already gone by then. Paralyzing Poliomyelitis. Quick, but terrible."

"I'm sorry." Mirabella twisted the toe of her shoe into the carpet. She knew what paralyze meant, that you couldn't move, but she didn't understand the other word. She would have asked him to explain it, but she thought it might make him even sadder, and he seemed so sad already.

"It was a long, long time ago." He gazed out the window, lost.

The wall clock ticked louder as silence settled over them. Mirabella felt the weight of lonely years hovering above the old man like a presence in the room. Like a ghost. She squirmed in her chair. "Would you tell me about it, I mean, about her?"

Dr. Benniton started, as if he'd forgotten she was there. He scratched his chin. "Ah, Sadie. I haven't spoken to anyone about her in years."

"I'm sorry." Mirabella started to stand.

Dr. Benniton waved her back onto the couch. "No, don't go. Just give me a moment to gather my thoughts." He rubbed his face, his hand shaking. "World War II was over. The economy was booming." His voice fell to a whisper. "We thought our lives were just beginning."

He leaned forward, his back stiff and hunched, and winced as he set the photo back onto the table. "She loved children. Wanted a whole passel of them." He gave her a weak smile. "Passel. That's an old out-of-date word that means a lot."

Mirabella didn't tell him she already knew what the word meant.

"I'd just hung out my shingle. That means I was just starting my medical practice. Oh, the world was rosy." His shoulders trembled. "There were several big polio epidemics in the country after the war, close to 20,000 people died each year from the disease. And in 1947 it spread here. A number of Sadie's students contracted the virus that summer. We didn't have a hospital, so we set up a makeshift ward in the school gymnasium. Sadie volunteered to help care for the patients." His eyes clouded and pain pinched his face.

"I tried to get her to stay away, but she insisted. Said if I could take the risk, then so could she. Besides, most of those kids were like her own."

"She took care of children?"

"She taught school. Fifth grade. She was good at it, too. All the children loved her." His face sagged. "And she loved them. There was no way I could keep her away when she found out they were ill." He shuddered. "I wish I could have talked her out of it. But she was headstrong. Had a mind of her own." A weak smile brushed across his face. "One of the many reasons I loved her was her passion, the way she cared for others."

Mirabella fidgeted with excitement. She could hardly wait to get back home and see if the ghost remembered any of the things Dr. Benniton was telling her.

"I'm sorry," Dr. Benniton said. "I must be boring you. We older folks forget sometimes that young people aren't as interested in our lives as we are."

"It isn't that," Mirabella said. "I'm really very interested. It's just that I have a lot of homework to do." And not all of it is mine, she thought, and felt herself flush with guilt and anger.

"I understand." He smiled at her, but it was a sad smile. "I hope you've learned enough for your article."

"Article?"

"Yes. The one you're writing. You will send me a copy when it's published, won't you?"

"Sure," Mirabella said, a little too quickly. She'd been so distracted she'd forgotten that she'd let him believe she was writing for the school paper. "But, um, I might have a few more questions." Mirabella hated lying to him. He was so nice, and he must be lonely here in this nursing home with no family to visit him. But if the ghost really had been his fiancée, Sadie, she might need an excuse to see him again. "Would it be all right if I visited you again sometime?"

He brightened. "Certainly, young lady. Always happy to oblige a budding young member of the press. Just check with Roger about visiting hours." He offered his hand to Mirabella.

She reached out and took it, and although his bony fingers looked fragile, his handshake was firm. "Thank you, Dr. Benniton. I'm really glad to have met you."

"And I am happy to have made your acquaintance, Miss Polidoro."

CHAPTER THIRTY-EIGHT

By the time Mirabella got home, it was dinnertime and there was no chance to talk to the ghost before she had to wash her hands and set the table. She ate so fast her mother reminded her three times to chew before she swallowed.

"You need to slow down, Mira. It isn't healthy to gulp your food. Remember, the digestive process begins in the mouth." It was one of her mom's favorite sayings.

"I know," Mirabella said, trying hard not to sound like she was talking back. She didn't want to start another argument with her mother. Today had already been bad enough without that. "But I have a lot of homework to do tonight." She thought again about Stacey and Erin. She wanted to tell her mother what had happened. But the two girls would only lie, and Mirabella's mother seemed so happy believing that she'd made friends. She'd probably find some way to blame Mirabella for the whole thing.

"So, what happened to this school being in the dark ages

and not challenging you enough?" Her mother took a sip of her water.

"I guess they were making it easy, so I could, um, adjust." Mirabella stared at her peas and carrots.

"Well, I suppose that's a good thing," her mother said. "But it's still no reason to wolf your dinner."

Mirabella concentrated on her plate for the rest of the meal, chewing each bite exactly thirty times before swallowing, which took forever. So did cleaning up afterward.

It was her turn to dry the dishes and her mother washed and rinsed every plate and cup and fork and knife, slowly and methodically, like they were surgical instruments that had to be super sanitized.

Mirabella leaned against the counter, waiting while her mother took an hour to wash a single plate. "Can I ask you a question, Mom?"

"About?" Her mother tilted the plate under the hot water to rinse away the soapsuds.

"A disease."

"Oh, a professional question. Let me put my nursing hat back on. Just so you know, I may send you a bill later, and my rates are not cheap," her mother said in her I'm-just-teasing-you voice.

Mirabella was quiet for a moment.

"Go ahead," her mother urged, a concerned look on her face.

"What happens when someone gets polio?"

"People don't get polio anymore. At least, not in this country. We have vaccines for it now." She handed the wet plate to Mirabella.

"I mean back before Jonas Salk developed the vaccine." Mirabella dried the plate and put it away. "What happened to them back then?"

Her mother thought about it. "Polio was pretty devastating," she said, scrubbing the soup pot until the copper bottom shone like a new piece of jewelry. "Why the sudden interest in polio?"

The soup ladle Mirabella was drying slipped from her grasp and clattered to the floor. She bent to pick it up, giving herself time to think. "I was doing a report for school and one of the people I interviewed had polio a long time ago, and now he's in Loring's nursing home."

"Loring's is an assisted living facility, not a nursing home." Her mother set the soup pot in the dish drainer and started to rewash the ladle.

"What's the difference?"

"Nursing homes are for people who need a lot of medical care and attention. An assisted living facility is more like an apartment building for people who need help doing things like cooking and who also need regular medical care." Her mother rinsed the flatware and placed it in the drainer. "It sounds like this person is actually one of the luckier victims of polio. A lot of people died from the disease. Many others were horribly crippled for life."

"Why did some people die and others get crippled?"

"Polio is caused by a virus," her mother explained. "Just like flu or chicken pox. Only, poliovirus attacks the nerves. It causes damage that disrupts the signals from the brain to the muscles in the body. So, some victims lose the ability to walk or use their arms." She drained the soapy water from the sink.

"But sometimes, the virus interrupts the nerves that help the body control the muscles required for breathing. Those people lost the ability to breathe on their own and had to be enclosed in large machines called iron lungs."

"Iron lungs?" Mirabella sorted the clean flatware into the drawer.

150

"An iron lung is a chamber that encloses everything except a person's head and neck. The chamber is sealed and then pressurized and depressurized, so the air inside it compresses and releases the person's chest. That causes air to be pulled in and pushed out of the lungs, just like regular breathing. Only, instead of the diaphragm and chest muscles, the changing air pressure inside the chamber does all the work. Nowadays, there are other ways to help a person breathe, so iron lungs aren't used much anymore."

Mirabella thought about Dr. Benniton and wondered if he'd always been in the assisted living facility. "So, if you got polio you either died or got crippled?"

"No. There have been many people who recovered almost completely, by using therapy and exercising to strengthen the muscles and retrain the nerves that weren't damaged or destroyed." Her mother finished scrubbing the sink. "But after a while, a lot of those people started getting sick again. It turned out that the type of therapy that helped them when they were first recovering from the disease, was exactly the wrong thing to do when the symptoms came back."

"What do you mean?"

"The therapy that worked while they were recovering from the virus included lots of exercise, walking and moving, and such." Water splashed up over the edge of the sink as she sprayed the sides to rinse away the cleanser. "But people whose symptoms return years later have what we call post-polio syndrome. Those people should do gentle exercise that doesn't wear them out or fatigue their muscles. They also need to rest more and try not to overexert themselves."

"But why would lots of exercise be good at first, and bad later?"

"It's a bit complicated," her mother said. "But basically, when the original nerves were damaged, some people's bodies adjusted by producing new nerve endings and the exercises increased the development of those cells. But years of excessive use causes stress to the original cells and the remaining nerves begin to break down."

"Why would they do that?" Mirabella wiped at the drips of water running down the front of the sink.

"The remaining nerves in their bodies, the ones that weren't damaged or that formed new nerve endings, had to do their own work and the work of the damaged nerves, too. So—"

"So they got worn out." Mirabella finished.

Like Dr. Benniton.

"Exactly."

"And if they work them more, instead of letting them rest, they wear them out even faster."

Her mom beamed at her. She always liked it when Mirabella figured out the answer to her own questions. "Did you know that one of the most famous presidents of the United States had polio?" she asked.

"Really? Which one?"

"Franklin Delano Roosevelt. His legs were left paralyzed after he contracted polio. He was the only US President in history to use a wheelchair."

After the dishes were put away and the table wiped, her mother actually offered to sweep the floor, even though it was Mirabella's turn. "But only because you have homework," she said, grabbing the broom and dustpan from the pantry. "And because you asked really good questions tonight, and listened to the answers."

"Thanks, mom!" Mirabella raced out of the kitchen and pounded up the stairs to her room.

CHAPTER THIRTY-NINE

"Hello?" Mirabella stood in the middle of her room, keeping her voice low so her mother wouldn't hear.

Nothing.

"Please come out," Mirabella said.

"Leave me be." The raspy voice came from far away.

"But I have something important to tell you."

A misty cloud emerged from the shadows and swirled before her, like steaming vapor from a pot of boiling water.

"I can hardly see you," Mirabella said.

"Let me fade in peace," the vapor hissed.

"No!" Mirabella shot a glance at her bedroom door and lowered her voice. "I have to talk to you."

The mist coalesced into a lumpy pillar of gray. "What is it you want?" It sounded weary.

"Sadie!" Mirabella said in desperation. "You need to listen."

"Sadie," the ghost echoed. Then, the apparition melted and

wheezed, flattened and fluttered, and slowly morphed into the form of the woman Mirabella had seen in Dr. Benniton's picture. She wasn't wearing a hat, and her hair was curled up in a long roll that ran around the back of her head with a pile of tight curls across her forehead. Instead of a skirt and jacket, she was wearing a dress with a wide lapel that buttoned all the way down and was belted at the waist. The dress swirled about her calves, making a bell shape, and the shoes were different, too. Higher heeled. But the face was the same one Dr. Benniton had stared at with longing.

It was true! Mirabella whooped for joy. The ghost really was Dr. Benniton's Sadie.

She bounded onto the bed and bounced on her knees. "We know who you are!" If she could have touched the ghost, she would have hugged her. She flopped off the bed and reached under the mattress for her journal, opening it to the place marked by the bright blue sticky note. The heading at the top of the page read: Ghost: Unfinished Business. It was followed by a numbered list. Mirabella checked off item number one, which simply read, "Who?" In the space beside the checkmark she wrote: Sadie, 1947, engaged to Dr. Benniton.

The ghost held out her arms and surveyed herself. "Is this what I'm supposed to look like?" She seemed surprised by her appearance.

Where before there had only been a vague outline of a person, there was now a young woman. Except for the slightly different clothes and the missing bouquet of flowers, the ghost looked just like a cloudy version of her picture. Or, rather, just like the picture of whom she had been in life.

Mirabella understood now why the ghost had never seemed to have legs. The full skirt swirled around Sadie's calves as she turned this way and that, trying to catch a glimpse of herself.

"It has to be." Mirabella laughed out loud. "Before I called you Sadie, you were all fuzzy, like an out of focus picture. But now, you almost look like a real person."

"Really?"

"Check the mirror, if you don't believe me."

The ghost floated over and settled onto the cushioned bench in front of the vanity.

"See?" Mirabella asked. "The blurriness is gone. Even your face has features now."

The ghost turned from side to side, staring at itself in the mirror. It frowned and Mirabella could see the wrinkle lines form on its, or rather her, forehead.

"You're her. You're Sadie."

"How can you be sure?"

"I look at you and I see the woman from the photo that Dr. Benniton showed me." Mirabella gazed at the ghost's reflection. "I can see the shape of her eyes. Your eyes."

Sadie's ghost flickered out.

"Wait. Come back!" Mirabella called out in frustration. "Why would you look exactly like that picture, if it wasn't you?"

Sadie's ghost suddenly reformed on the other side of the room. "If we know who I am, then why am I still here?"

Mirabella exhaled in relief. "Have you tried to leave?"

"That's where I went just now." Sadie floated over to the corner and sank down onto the overstuffed chair. "But it didn't work."

The disarray of library books and discarded clothes stacked in the chair was visible through her opaque form, and Mirabella had to force herself not to stare. "I don't know." She pulled her legs up to her chest and wrapped her arms around her knees.

They sat in silence for a long while, Sadie drooping in the easy chair, Mirabella wrapped in thought. There must be something else they needed to do. Something that had to do with Dr. Benniton. He had never gotten married. So, he must have loved Sadie very much.

And Sadie had clung to the house where they were going to live. Why? Because she wanted to be with him? Because she couldn't bear to leave him? Because she still loved him?

Mirabella wondered if her father might have tried to stay if he'd loved her and her mother enough. She shook the question away. The book about ghosts hadn't said anything about love, only unfinished business with the living.

Maybe Sadie had wanted to find a way to tell Dr. Benniton something, but she couldn't because he had never moved into the house. He'd sold it and gone on with his life. Only, he hadn't really moved on any more than Sadie had.

"What if . . ." Mirabella said, speaking her thoughts aloud.

Sadie stirred in the corner and a chill breeze wafted across the room and caressed Mirabella's cheek. Goose bumps rose on her skin and she rubbed her arms. "What if it's something you still need to do?"

"But what can I do? I can hardly manage to hover on a chair well enough to pretend I'm sitting on it. If I let go—" Sadie let herself sink down through the chair and half way into the floor before Mirabella stopped her with a hiss.

"What if my mother is in the room below us?"

"So?" Sadie wheezed. "What if she is?"

"She might see you!"

"I don't think so." Sadie floated back up. "I told you. In all the time I've been here, you're the only one who has ever seen me."

"Are you sure?"

"Of course I'm not," Sadie grumbled, and her form shivered and flexed before returning to the now familiar figure of a young woman in old-fashioned clothes. "I'm not even sure if this Dr. Benniton is why I'm still here."

"I'm sorry. I didn't mean to upset you." At least she hadn't disappeared this time. Mirabella tapped her fingertips together while she considered the problem.

"Well, you can move small things," she said, finally. "I've seen you do that."

"I suppose," Sadie agreed. "But those things were mostly just tricks, moving the air, or moving items that have personal energy attached to them. Like your journal." She looked away and refused to meet Mirabella's gaze. "That's all I can remember ever being able to do."

"You obviously chose this house for a reason." Mirabella bobbed up and began pacing the floor. "I bet it's because he had it built for you and . . . and you thought he'd move in here. Only he didn't and then . . . then you got stuck." She paced back the other way. "Because you never got to tell him, or show him, or whatever it was you needed to do."

"But if that's true—"

"If that's true," Mirabella spun around to face Sadie, bouncing up and down on the balls of her feet. "Then all we have to do is get him to come to the house, so you can tell him what you need to, and then you should be able to leave before the house is torn down."

"Oh, that's wonderful!" Sadie rose up out of the chair and fluttered across the room toward Mirabella, her full skirt billowing around her legs. "Or is it?"

For a moment, Mirabella thought about not telling Sadie what she knew. She didn't want to lose her only real friend. Didn't want to face that kind of loss. Again. "It is," she said finally, resolved to do whatever was necessary to keep the ghost from a potentially horrible fate. "Absolutely."

"How will you get him to come here?"

Mirabella crossed her arms. "We'll think of something."

CHAPTER FORTY

The kitchen door was flung open before Mirabella had a chance to turn the doorknob. Her mother stood glaring at her. "Where have you been?" She was wearing her you're-in-the-deepest-kind-of-trouble look. "You are so grounded!" Her mother stood back from the door to let her pass by into the house.

Mirabella's face felt thin. Like her skull was being squeezed in giant hands and all the blood was being pushed out of her head, which had started to throb.

"I was doing homework. At the library."

Her mother's lips were moving, but a whooshing sound filled Mirabella's ears and she could barely hear her mother's angry voice above the rushing noise. She gripped the strap of her messenger bag till it dug into the palm of her hand, twisting her fingers into the rough canvas, and tried to focus on her mother's voice. Tried to make sense of the sounds. She pinned her attention on them until they began to sound like words, then phrases, and finally sentences that drifted through to her like an old plow though a thick snow bank, and her jaw dropped open.

"Don't look at me like that, young lady. Your little friends told the principal everything. I thought that spending time with decent girls like that would help you. But, no. You had to go and drag them into your rotten little pranks."

Mirabella shuffled to the table, flinching when the door slammed shut behind her.

Her mother marched across the kitchen. "I cannot believe, that after all I said, you went ahead and started playing these terrible tricks on people again." She put her hand on her forehead, as if it hurt her. "And this prank, it's beyond anything. It's the worst thing you've ever done!"

Mirabella's jaw tightened. "I didn't do anything."

"Don't you dare lie to me," her mother warned, her voice rising to a shout. "We'll be lucky if that poor girl's parents don't push to have you expelled from school. How could you joke about such a horrible thing as hurting a defenseless pet?" Her shoulders dropped and she stared at Mirabella. A hurt expression painted her face. "Haven't I taught you anything?"

Mirabella felt the blood rushing through her hands and vibrating in her head. "Hurt?" Her voice rasped in her own ears, like the wind blowing through a field of dry weeds. "What do you mean, hurt a pet?"

"Don't act innocent with me, Mirabella Roxanne Polidoro. You know exactly what I mean. Sending that poor girl a note telling her that someone was going to harm her little dog is the most awful thing you could have done." Her mother sagged into a chair. "I can't imagine. That poor little girl. She must have been frightened out of her mind." She leaned across the table and glared at Mirabella. "Did you get the reaction you were looking for?"

Mirabella's knees felt weak. She clutched at the back of a kitchen chair, trying to work things through. Then her mind opened up like a door yawning wide. Stacey and Erin! It had to be them. Stacey had warned her there would be a lesson for not getting their homework done.

"Mom," she said in her most adult voice. "It's not what you think. I would never do anything like that."

Her mother's mouth turned into a thin line that stretched across her face. "Mira."

Mirabella heard the warning in the way her mother spoke her name. Tears pushed at the backs of her eyes. This was all wrong. "But Mom, you have to let me explain."

"Explain what, Mirabella? How you need to know how people will react in a crisis? How you can't ask them how they'll react because they don't know?" She stood up and the chair screeched backward across the floor. "And don't tell me you read those things somewhere. I know who put those ideas into your head, and if he were here right now, I'd give him a piece of my mind!"

It was too much. Mirabella felt all the anger well up inside her, rushing from her feet to her head like some sick geyser of blackness. "Well, he's not here," she heard herself yelling. "And he never will be. Because you already told him what you thought!"

Her mother stared at her, stunned.

Mirabella didn't care. With a loud sob, she heaved her messenger bag onto her shoulder. "Things couldn't be any worse, and it's all your fault! If you hadn't made us move here in the first place, none of this would be happening. If you and Daddy had never separated, he'd probably still be alive and everything would be fine!"

She rushed from the kitchen and ran up the stairs to her room.

It wasn't fine. And it never would be.

`

CHAPTER FORTY-ONE

Mirabella sank back into her pillows. She drew her knees up so she could balance her notebook against them as she wrote. She hated this assignment. Two pages on the Louisiana Purchase! Who cared?

School had been horrible. Stacey had smirked at her every time she saw her. She reminded Mirabella of one of those grinning chimpanzees they put on joke birthday cards. It would have been funny if Mirabella weren't so worried that Stacey might be planning something even worse than the nasty prank she'd already blamed on Mirabella.

Completely grounded. She wasn't even allowed to go to the library. If she needed books to do her homework, she had to ask her mother to pick them up for her.

Worse, her mother had the neighbors watching and checking up on her to make sure she came straight home from school. She needed to see Dr. Benniton, and soon. But there was no way her mother would let her go anywhere, not even to the assisted living home.

She ripped the page from her notebook and crumpled it in her hand, tossing it at the wastebasket. It went in and she sighed, wondering where Sadie was. Not that it really mattered. Sadie couldn't help, and Mirabella didn't want to crush the poor ghost's hope. Ever since Mirabella had helped her to remember who she was, the spirit had been brighter and less inclined to become upset, blink out, and disappear.

How could Mirabella tell her that her worst fear was about to come true? That she was on the verge of wandering the earth alone, with no home, until she forgot herself and everything she once knew. Or, like the book said, tormenting some poor kid. No wonder the possibility horrified Sadie. She had loved kids so much she had risked and lost her life trying to help the children of Robertsville.

Mirabella shoved the notebook away and leaped from the bed. Being grounded was bad enough, but being grounded when there was so much she needed to do was a nightmare, one she couldn't wake up from because she wasn't asleep in the first place.

There had to be a way to see Dr. Benniton, talk to him. She couldn't explain about Sadie over the phone—not that she was allowed to use the phone anyway—and a note would just sound crazy:

Dear Dr. Benniton,

The ghost of your dead fiancée is living in my Aunt Clovinia's house and would like to speak with you. If she doesn't see you soon, she will end up roaming the earth with no memories until she torments a small child. So, please come see her right away.

Your friend,
Mirabella Polidoro

Right. Like that didn't sound insane. He'd probably call her mother to suggest she take Mirabella to a psychiatrist. Then her mother would re-ground her for what she called "pulling another prank."

Think! she told herself, but she ransacked her brain, sifting through one idea after another, without finding a solution to her primary problem. She had to talk to Dr. Benniton, and it had to be in person. There was no way to sneak out of the house when her mother was home. Mirabella was allowed to study, or to read, but she had to do it at the kitchen table where her mom could see her and watch her every move. She called it "fish-bowling." Mirabella hated it. She couldn't even leave when her mother wasn't home. The neighbors were under orders to immediately call her mother if Mirabella so much as stuck her head outside the house.

She threw herself onto the bed, shoved her face into her pillow, and roared her frustration into its plump softness. A cold breeze prickled down her back and she raised her head.

"Sadie?"

"You seem upset." The ghost's voice caressed her like a cool wind.

A shudder ran through Mirabella. She wanted so much to tell Sadie how she felt, to have her listen to her problems and care. But how could she? How could she tell Sadie, who had been a schoolteacher, that she was helping other students cheat? And how could she take away the poor ghost's newfound hope of being free by telling her that Mirabella couldn't help her anymore because she'd gotten into trouble?

She needed to tell Sadie she hadn't been able to talk to Dr.

Benniton, but she had to do it without giving away any details. Sitting up, she pulled her knees to her chin and wrapped her arms around her legs. "My mom's mad at me," she said, watching Sadie's reaction. "She grounded me. So I haven't been able go and to see Mr.—your fiancé. That's why he hasn't come to see you, yet."

Sadie drifted to and fro, but said nothing.

The silence scratched at Mirabella. She waited, expecting Sadie to begin flickering or simply disappear. But the ghost continued to sway in the air. No blinking. No fading. Just the tiniest movement, like a leaf on a tree swayed by the lightest of air currents.

"I've tried to think of something," Mirabella blurted. "But she's even got me under neighborhood watch. I can't go anywhere, except school, unless she's right there with me. Like when she takes me to do the grocery shopping." She hung her head, using her knees to wipe at the tears that had gathered in the corners of her eyes.

After a few seconds, she jerked her head up. "I could ask her to take me to Loring's to see him." She gazed at the air in front of her.

"Why don't you?" Sadie asked.

Mirabella shook her head. "She'd be right there. How can I tell him about you with her sitting there? She'll think it's a—a prank."

"Why would she think that?"

"Because it's an unbelievable story. It's going to be hard enough to explain it to Dr. Benniton. Even with the things you've remembered, it's going to be difficult to make him believe me." Mirabella glanced at Sadie. "And there's another reason."

"Another reason?"

"Yes." She gnawed at her thumbnail, trying to figure out a

way to get her mother to take her to see Dr. Benniton. If she told her she needed to see him to ask some follow-up questions for her report, she'd probably agree to take her. Schoolwork was always rated a priority, even when she was in trouble.

"What is it?"

Mirabella grabbed her notebook and fished around on the wrinkled bedspread for her pen. She needed to think of some questions to ask Dr. Benniton, so her mother wouldn't be suspicious. And she'd better write some sort of report in case her mother wanted to see what she'd written so far. "I'd rather not talk about it right now, okay?" she said. "I mean, we're on a deadline and I've got a lot of work to do before I can ask my mom to take me to Loring's."

CHAPTER FORTY-TWO

"Ghosts and spirits. Bah!" Dr. Benniton waved a feeble hand as if pushing away the thought. "I'm a man of science."

This was not going well. She seemed to be getting nowhere and her mother might be back at any moment.

Mirabella had managed to talk her mother into letting her visit Dr. Benniton, but of course she'd insisted on going along to make sure Mirabella didn't cause any more trouble. Mirabella had asked her prepared questions and wrote down the answers slowly, often asking him to repeat things to stall for time. She had nearly run out of questions when Roger had stuck his head into the room.

"Roger," Dr. Benniton said. "Have you met my young friend's mother?"

"I'm afraid I haven't had the pleasure." Roger crossed the room and stuck out his hand.

Mirabella's mother stood to shake hands with him.

"Nice scrubs," Roger said. "Are you a nurse?"

Mirabella's mother glanced down at herself. She was wearing a pair of black scrub pants with a black and white polka dotted tunic and her white cross trainers. She beamed up at Roger. "R.N. I work at Dr. Worth's clinic."

"Dr. Worth is a good M.D.," Roger said. "Several of the clients here are patients of his."

"Oh, that's right," she said. "Tuesdays and Thursdays. That's why he's out of the clinic on those afternoons."

"Yes," Roger said. "He's been coming here twice a week for years. Just about ever since the place opened."

"When was that?" Mirabella's mother asked.

"The facility was built in the 1990s," he said. "Would you like to take a quick tour?"

"I wouldn't want to keep you from your work." Mirabella's mother gave her a stern look. "And I really should stay here with my daughter."

"It's time for my break." Roger smiled. "Mirabella and Dr. Benniton will be fine till we get back. They're practically old friends now."

Dr. Benniton nodded and waved them on. "You two go on. We'll be fine."

Mirabella was amazed when her mother finally said yes. Although she tossed Mirabella one of her don't-you-dare-go-anywhere-or-do-anything-you-shouldn't-while-I'm-gone looks before following Roger out of the room.

Once alone with Dr. Benniton, Mirabella had started off with care, hoping to bring up the subject slowly, but when she'd started talking about seeing Sadie's spirit in the house, Dr. Benniton had stopped her with a loud snort.

"Bunk. Plain bunk." He leaned forward and squinted at Mirabella. "Is this what you've been working up to? Eh?" He frowned and wagged a bony finger at her. "You should be ashamed, young lady, leading a man to believe you care what he thinks or says, then trying to get him to say something you can laugh at or video tape and post all over the Internet."

"No," Mirabella protested, trying to find a way to repair the damage her words had done. "That's not it at all. I just wondered what you thought."

He grimaced in pain and sat back suddenly. "I'll tell you what I think," he said, his breathing ragged. "I think you should go home and leave me alone. That's what I think."

"But—"

His face hardened. "How would you like me to call your father and tell him you've been pestering a poor old man with impertinent questions?"

Mirabella vaulted to her feet, her hands shaking so hard her pen and notepad slipped from her grip and clattered to the floor. "You can't call my father."

"What makes you think I can't?" He grumbled. "I'm disabled, not incapable."

"You can't call him," Mirabella said, her voice cracking. "You can't call him, because he's dead. Just like your Sadie. Only I'll never get a chance to see him again."

She stooped and picked up her things and started to leave, but stopped in the doorway and looked back at his stunned face. "But if I had the chance," she said, holding back a sob, "I wouldn't just sit in my room feeling sorry for myself. I'd do whatever it took to talk to him one last time. That's what I'd do." She heaved the door open and ran out of the room and down the hallway.

She nearly collided with Roger in the lobby.

"Whoa, there." He held out his hands like a traffic cop signaling the drivers to stop. "Are you all right?" he asked.

"I . . . I'm fine." Mirabella forced her voice to an even tone. "Where's my mom?"

A quick blush leaped across Roger's face. "She's in the

169

ladies room, cleaning up. I'm afraid I spilled coffee on her during our tour of the cafeteria."

Mirabella felt her lower lip tremble and she turned away from him.

"Why don't you have a seat out here in the waiting area," he said, kindly. "I'm sure your mom will be right out."

Mirabella nodded and slouched down into one of the chairs that faced the front windows, willing her eyes to stay dry.

CHAPTER FORTY-THREE

"Try, Sadie." Mirabella knelt on the bed as Sadie drifted back and forth across the room, the ghostly version of pacing. Odd to think of a spirit being full of nervous energy. Especially, Mirabella thought, when energy was almost all a ghost was made of.

Or was it? She sat back on her heels and thought about it. She'd have to add that to her research list for the future. "There were roses, right? Yellow ones? And you were engaged. You remember that now, don't you?" She glanced at the notes she'd made in her journal.

"Yes." Sadie continued to pace. "I think so."

"You were!" Mirabella insisted. "He said so." She climbed off the bed and stepped in front of the ghost, stopping its progress.

"I guess. If you say so."

"He has your picture. And you look just like her, I mean it." Mirabella huffed out her breath. "I mean you." She shook

171

her head. "All you have to do is remember something that only you and he would know. Like your favorite color. Or his favorite color."

Sadie drifted away from her, wringing her pale hands and shaking her head. "I want to," she moaned. "I want to remember so much. But it's all so faint and far away. Like a distant mountain on a misty day. The shape is there, but I can't make out any of the details!"

Mirabella crossed her arms over her chest and tapped her foot. She wanted to be encouraging, but she was getting frustrated. "There has to be something. Something meaningful. Something—"

"Sentimental!" Sadie said.

"Sure," Mirabella said. "Something sentimental. That would—"

Sadie flitted around the room like a giant moth. "No," she said. "No, no, no, no, no. Not something sentimental. Sentimental. Just sentimental."

Mirabella sat up and watched Sadie float across the floor humming something.

"Sentimental reasons!" Sadie swirled around the room once more, and then began to sing, "I love you, for sentimental reasons. I hope you do believe me. I'll give you my heart."

She glowed with light and swayed in time with the song. "I remember," she said. "I remember. It was our song, and Nat King Cole sang it."

She stopped in midair, then melted to the floor and began to weep. "It would have been our wedding dance."

Sadie shuddered and sobbed. Terrible moans tore from her. Mirabella expected her to disappear, the way she usually did when she was upset, but instead Sadie's human-looking form began to separate in sad tatters that scattered across the floor like floating dust bunnies.

Mirabella's heart crumpled at the sight of Sadie's sorrow, yet a part of her was overjoyed. Here was some information she could use to convince Dr. Benniton she was telling the truth.

"Sadie?" She knelt beside what was left of the indistinct apparition. "Please don't cry." She watched the cloudlike mist that floated in the air around her, wondering how it must feel to be able to fall apart like that. Was it frightening? Or was it a relief to let go and allow yourself to be swept away by the slightest air current?

"I thought you'd be happy to finally remember." Mirabella scratched at a peeling spot of floor varnish with her thumbnail. Her heart ached for her friend. "At least now maybe he'll believe me when I tell him who you are."

The sobbing grew quieter, then stopped, and Mirabella watched in wonder as the small wisps swirled back to where Sadie had collapsed, and the ghost rematerialized in the shape of the young woman in Dr. Benniton's faded photograph.

Sadie looked up at her. "Do you really think so?" There was sadness in her face, but her voice held a hopeful quaver.

Mirabella felt odd, sitting on the floor and reassuring an adult. Although, she wondered why it was that, and not the fact that she was sitting on the floor with a ghost, that made her feel awkward. She wished that she could touch Sadie, hold her hand or give her a reassuring hug. She'd never understood before how much people seemed to depend on touch for comfort. She realized suddenly how her mother must have felt when she'd refused to let her hug her or comfort her after her father had died. The guilt that washed through her made her wince and wish she could fade the way that Sadie could.

"Will he come?" Sadie asked her. "Will he really come to see me?"

Mirabella twisted her fingers together and studied the pale

gray eyes that pleaded with her to say yes. "I hope so," she said, unable to lie to those hopeful eyes. "I'll do everything I can to convince him."

She forced herself to sound confident, but a worry nagged at her. What if he still didn't believe her? What if he didn't come and the house was destroyed with Sadie trapped inside? What then?

Mirabella couldn't bear to think about how horrible that would be.

CHAPTER FORTY-FOUR

Sneaking over to Loring's after school was way out of bounds, but Mirabella had to risk it for Sadie's sake. The receptionist greeted her with a professional-looking smile. "Can I get something for you, honey?" she asked, her mouth wrinkling up at the corners as she looked up from her computer.

"I'd like to see Dr. Benniton." Mirabella said, in a whisper.

"Pardon me, what was that?" The woman cupped her hand near her ear where a pink plastic hearing aid fit so snugly that Mirabella hadn't noticed it.

"I'd like to see Dr. Benniton," she repeated more loudly.

"He won't see you," said a voice from behind her. Mirabella turned to see Roger, coming in from outside. He wore a red and black leather jacket and held a matching motorcycle helmet in the crook of his left arm.

He shook his head. "I don't know what you said to him, but after you left the other day he was mumbling something about how foolish old men, who let people take advantage of them, get what they deserve. Then he told me not to let you back in."

Mirabella's heart buckled. Dr. Benniton had been one of the few people who had been kind to her since she'd moved to this rotten town, and now he wouldn't even see her. What would happen to Sadie? She stared down the hallway toward Dr. Benniton's room.

"He doesn't get any other visitors." Roger set his helmet on the receptionist's desk and unzipped his jacket. "His health has been declining for such a long while and your visits seemed to be just what he needed. But now . . ." His voice trailed off.

Mirabella felt the blood rising to her face. She didn't want to tell Roger what had happened. She'd never yelled at a grownup before, except her mom, and that had always gotten her into big trouble. She looked up. Roger was watching her closely.

"What happened? he asked. "You two seemed to be getting along so well."

"We sort of had an argument." Mirabella twisted her fingers together.

"It must have been a real doozie." Roger picked up his helmet and gloves. "I've never seen him act the way he has the last couple of days. He won't even do his physical therapy. Says it isn't worth the trouble and not to waste my time on him."

"I'm sorry," Mirabella said. "I really am. But I really need to talk to him, to explain."

Roger shook his head and frowned. "No," he said. "I'm sorry, but I can't let you see him. I have to respect his wishes." He tossed his gloves inside his helmet and walked past the reception desk and down the hall.

It was just too terrible. She'd promised Sadie she'd talk to him, try and persuade him. How could she do that, if he wouldn't even see her? "Wait!" she called after Roger.

The receptionist jerked her head up at the sound and gave her a disapproving look. But Mirabella didn't care. She had to try one last thing. "Please," she pleaded.

Roger halted and turned to face her. His voice was stern. "I told you I can't let you in," he said.

"You'll need to leave now," the receptionist said, making a shooing motion with her hand.

Mirabella pretended not to notice her. "Could you at least give him a note for me?" She pulled out her notepad. "He won't have to see me, so you'll still be respecting his wishes." She rummaged for a pen, her gaze on Roger.

Roger waited for her to finish writing, then took the note from her. "I'll give it to him," he said. "But I can't promise he'll read it."

Mirabella waited anxiously in the lobby while Roger took her note to Dr. Benniton. Had she gotten the words right? She tried to sit in one of the bright-colored lobby chairs, but couldn't stop fidgeting.

She stood by the reception counter and leaned over it to look down the hallway, but the woman scowled and Mirabella stepped back. After that, the woman raised her head to glare at Mirabella every few seconds, as if she thought Mirabella would try to sneak down the hallway if she took her eyes off her for more than a moment.

It seemed like forever before Roger returned. He didn't say a word. He didn't have to. The look on his face was enough.

She had failed.

CHAPTER FORTY-FIVE

"What will we do, now?"

"More research."

Sadie soared over the bed. "Is that what you're doing, here?" She pointed at the papers and books scattered across the covers.

"No!" Mirabella scrambled to the bed and scraped the papers together into an awkward pile. "This is just homework." She opened the Hello Kitty folder and jammed the loose pages into it.

"Homework?"

"Yes." Mirabella hugged the folder to her chest.

"Then why does it have someone else's name on it?" Sadie demanded.

"It . . . I . . . that is . . . "

"You're doing someone else's homework?" The ghost put her hands on her hips and stared down at Mirabella, hovering over her like an angry balloon.

Mirabella sat on the bed and bent over her books, trying to appear as if she was concentrating, but the ghost continued to hover.

"I'm trying to read," Mirabella said.

Sadie stayed by the bed, unwavering. Mirabella focused on her book and tried to ignore her.

"What do you think your mother would say if she knew you were doing someone else's homework?" Sadie finally asked.

"She wouldn't care," Mirabella said weakly. She knew it was a lie, but maybe the ghost would accept it and leave her alone.

"I don't believe that. In fact, I'm sure she would care, and that she wouldn't approve."

Mirabella kept her eyes stuck to the pages of her book. "How do you know?"

Sadie fluttered around the bed, blinking in and out. "I just do," she said.

"Why are you so angry?" Mirabella put aside her book and watched the ghost flit back and forth across the room in rapid bursts.

"Because doing someone else's schoolwork is tantamount to cheating. And we do not tolerate cheaters in this school." Sadie stopped right in front of Mirabella and crossed her arms.

"This isn't a school. It's my room and I can do what I want."

"I don't like your attitude, young lady. And I will not tolerate backtalk from a student."

"But I'm not your student." Mirabella gave Sadie a quizzical look. "I thought we were friends," Mirabella said.

Sadie shook her head and for a moment her face was a blurry gray cloud. Then her features reformed and she let out an odd whispery "Oooh." She floated down to floor level.

179

"Yes, we are," she said. "At least, I believe we are."

"Then, why can't you just leave me alone?" Mirabella slammed her book shut.

"Because we are friends," Sadie said. "And I think you should tell me why you would do such a thing."

"Because," Mirabella said.

Sadie waited.

"Because I promised I would?" Mirabella was too embarrassed to tell Sadie the truth.

"But why would you make such a promise?"

Mirabella dug at her cuticles, hoping Sadie would forget about it, but the ghost waited, patient and quiet. It figures, Mirabella thought. She's just like an adult. When you want them to forget something, they never do.

Mirabella kept rubbing her fingers across the beds of her nails. She might as well tell her. It wasn't like Sadie could tell anyone else, much less Mirabella's mother.

"They made me promise to do their work," she said. "They said they'd get me into trouble if I didn't."

"Who are they?" Sadie coaxed her.

"Some girls at school," she said. Then she thought about it. It had only been Stacey who had really threatened her. Erin just went along with everything and did whatever Stacey told her to.

"But you know it's wrong, don't you?" Sadie slid closer to her and Mirabella felt the ghost's chill. Goosebumps formed on her arms and she rubbed at them.

"I guess so. But I can't say anything to my mother. She and I were almost getting along, and then Stacey told that lie about me!" She thought about all the times since her father's death, when she and her mother had had nothing to say to one another, unless her mother was scolding or nagging her about something. But lately, they'd started actually having conversations again. Talking about other things, like polio and presidents. Real conversations. She'd thought about telling her what was going on at school. About Stacey and Erin. About the homework. But she hadn't wanted her mother to get mad and stop talking to her again. Then Stacey had gone and messed everything up, blaming her for that stupid prank. Now, things were worse than ever.

"You need to tell her," Sadie said. "You need to tell her everything." She suddenly swept across the room, a blur of misty gray. She seemed agitated.

"What's wrong?" Mirabella asked.

"What's wrong?" Sadie nearly shrieked. "What's wrong?" she repeated. "You need to tell her what you're doing. You need to tell her before it's too late!"

Mirabella backed away on the bed. She'd never seen Sadie upset like this before. Usually she just blinked out, flashed a few times and disappeared.

Sadie blurred, becoming blobby like she'd been when Mirabella had first seen her. She floated around the room, faster and faster. She stopped in front of Mirabella and hung in the air like an ugly dark cloud. "If you don't tell her, I'll find a way to!" Sadie boomed so loud Mirabella was sure her mother really would hear her.

"No." Mirabella stomped her foot. "It's my room, and if you don't like what I'm doing, then you can leave."

The ghost suddenly put her hands to her face. Then, without another word, she disappeared.

CHAPTER FORTY-SIX

Mirabella hugged her pillow to her and sobbed into its softness. Nothing had gone right for her since moving here. Nothing. Even the one thing she was sure she could do, had failed. And now, no one was speaking to her. Not Sadie. Or Dr. Benniton. And her mom was still so mad she only talked at her, telling her what to do. Or what not to do.

Stacey was demanding that she do her homework for every single class, and now she wanted the answers to all the tests, too. Mirabella was afraid to look her teachers in the eye, especially Mr. Klutter, who had been so nice to her. She wanted to hide, to stay away from everyone. She felt like a criminal.

She pulled her journal out from under her mattress and thumbed through it, looking for a blank page. Words flitted past as she flipped the pages and she stopped when she saw the lyrics to the song that had belonged to Sadie and Dr. Benniton.

I love you, for sentimental reasons.
I hope you do believe me. I'll give you my heart.
I love you, and you alone were meant for me.
Please give your loving heart to me. And say we'll never part.

She shook her head. Did people really believe that stuff? That they could stay together and be in love forever? She ripped the page from the book, wadded it into a tight ball and heaved it at the trash can. It went straight in and stayed there.

She took a deep breath and began to write, scratching deep into the page with her purple pen, asking herself questions, the way her father used to ask her when things just didn't seem to be going right. Whether it was a homework project, or a problem with someone at school, her father had always been there to listen. But he'd also helped her figure out a lot of things without giving her the answers.

"Remember, Mira, the best way to figure out where you're going, is to take your bearings. Figure out where you are and where you've been," he'd told her. "That way, if you find yourself on the wrong path, you can make a course correction." He'd taught her that this logic applied not only to hiking and star maps, but also to life.

She numbered the left side of the page from one to ten. Then she went down the page and listed the things that were wrong.

1) Mom is angry about stuff I didn't do and won't listen to me.

2) Sadie is still lost and now she won't talk to me.

3) I found Dr. Benniton, but he doesn't believe me

about Sadie.

4) I can't. No, I won't talk to Mr. Klutter. I can't tell him I've been cheating in his class. And my other classes, too.

5) Stacey is getting me into trouble by telling lies.

6) My grades are falling.

7) I feel terrible.

8) Why?

9) Because mom is mad at me, and Sadie won't talk to me.

10) Why?

Because she thinks I'm irresponsible, and that I don't think about what I'm doing.

Why?

Because she thinks I pulled that stupid prank on that Monica girl, even though I don't even know her.

Why?

Because Stacey told her I did.

Why?

Because I didn't do exactly what Stacey wanted me to.

Why?

Because it's wrong.

And because Dad would be totally disappointed.

By the time she finished her list, huge tears were cascading onto the page and the letters had smeared into wet purple splotches.

CHAPTER FORTY- SEVEN

Mirabella pressed her cheek to the window, her breath making a cloud of fog on the frozen glass. She drew a big loopy flower in the fog and frowned. In two days, she and her mother would move across town into the small duplex her mother had found. She'd still have to go to stupid Jerkemiah Flushing Elementary. Dr. Benniton hated her, and had no one to visit him. And, worst of all, she hadn't helped Sadie. In fact, she'd only made things worse by making her remember who she was and telling her what her fate would be.

She wiped away the sad flower, peered out at the street and sighed, watching as a blue and white taxi pulled up in front of the house. The cab driver got out of the car and opened the trunk. He pulled out a metal walker with two small wheels and set it beside the back door of the car. Then, he opened the back door and helped his passenger climb out of the back seat.

A bent figure took hold of the handles on the walker and leaned over it, pushing it toward the curb in small jerks, one wobbly step at a time. The taxi cab driver walked slowly beside the man and helped him to lift his metal walker up onto the sidewalk before getting back into the car and driving away.

The old man hunched over the walker on the sidewalk, tilting his head to gaze up at the house, and Mirabella recognized his face.

Dr. Benniton! He'd come!

"Sadie!" she yelled. "Sadie, he's here! He came!" Mirabella hopped on the bed and spun around, calling out for Sadie in her loudest voice, but there was no response. "Sadie! You have to come out. He's really here." Mirabella leaped off the bed and ran back to the window. Outside, Dr. Benniton inched his way toward the house. His back was hunched and his head down. Every step seemed to take him forever. *Push. Step. Step. Push. Step. Step.*

"Oh, Sadie. Where are you?" Mirabella searched the room, hoping to see a spot of mist or swirling haze. She waved her arms around, feeling for frigid air, but she found none. She glanced back down at the front walk.

Dr. Benniton was half way to the porch. He'd never manage the steps. She had to go down and help him, but she didn't want to go without Sadie. Why wouldn't she show herself? Could she so easily have forgotten in just a few days all that she'd remembered in the last few weeks? No! It was too horrible to think that, after all they had done, Sadie might have truly faded beyond remembrance.

A last glance out the window told her that Dr. Benniton had reached the porch and was attempting to lift his walker up onto the lowest step.

Mirabella headed toward the hall, then turned and faced the room. "Sadie, you come out and see him." She demanded in her best this-is-how-my-mom-says-it-when-she-really-means-it voice. "This is what you've waited for. This is why you're still here. After all these years, I would think you'd want to see the man who never married anyone else because he was so in love with you."

Nothing.

"I'm going downstairs to let him in. You had better be here when I get back!" Mirabella stomped down the hallway and pounded down the stairs. As she reached the front entryway, the doorbell rang and she started. She'd thought she'd reach the door long before Dr. Benniton could get to it.

Her hands shook as she turned the worn brass knob and pulled open the heavy door.

Dr. Benniton stood panting on the landing, flushed, his breath puffing out in steamy clouds.

"Well, I'm here." He huffed and wheezed so hard, Mirabella worried he might pass out.

"Are you all right, Dr. Benniton?"

"What? No, I'm not all right," he grumped. "I'm a crazy old man. Like to kill myself in order to be the butt of some practical joke."

"It's not a joke, Dr. Benniton. Honest." Mirabella pulled the door open wide to accommodate his walker and stood aside so he could enter the house. His trembling hands gripped his walker.

"Can I get you a glass of water or something?" Mirabella offered.

He wheezed as he pushed and shuffled into the house. "I did not come all this way for a glass of water."

He paused, just far enough inside to allow her to close the door. Then he raised his head as high as he could and scanned the room. He seemed to be looking for something, staring first in one direction and then another, taking in every nook and cranny of the old place.

"It's just like we pictured it. Just the way she wanted it."

His shoulders drooped and he let out a heavy sigh, his eyes bright with unshed tears. "I never saw it finished. Never could bear to come inside after . . ."

"I'm sorry, Dr. Benniton. I'm so sorry." Mirabella's voice cracked. "But, she needed you to come. She—"

"Poppycock!" he hollered. "Young lady, I don't know what you're up to. The only reason I came was to see the old place for myself before I die." He frowned. "Now I've seen it, I'll be going." Then he pushed his walker in a circle, metal thumping hard against the wooden floorboards as he turned toward the door.

"Wait!" Mirabella rushed around him and put her back to the door. "Please, don't go yet," she pleaded. "Please."

The old man leaned over his walker and sucked in a long wheezy breath. His eyes, when he looked at Mirabella, were red-rimmed and filled with sadness. But he stood quietly for a moment, assessing her.

"You poor child," he whispered. "You truly do believe the stories you've been telling me?" His hands shuddered on the handles of the walker and he shook his head. "I don't know why you have so powerful a need to believe in things of that kind, Mirabella, but there are no such things as ghosts." His voice was thick and he paused to clear his throat. "As much as we'd like the spirits of our dear departed to visit us, it just isn't possible. I'm afraid you've let your imagination run away with you."

Mirabella sagged against the door. Her imagination? But it seemed so real! Could it have been all in her head? Had Sadie been nothing more than an imaginary friend?

Dr. Benniton reached a shaking hand into his pocket and brought out a handkerchief and blew his nose. "And, silly old romantic that I am . . ." He smiled weakly as he stuffed the handkerchief back into his pocket. "I wanted to believe you."

"But—"

"Please, no more ghost stories." He waved a hand at her. "But I think I will have that glass of water, now. If you don't mind."

Mirabella was stunned. Was that why Sadie hadn't appeared when she'd called, because she had never really been there? Except in Mirabella's mind? Was that the reason no one else had ever seen the ghost? Because there wasn't one? She headed toward the kitchen, her feet dragging across the old floor, and Dr. Benniton scuffled behind her.

She tried to admit to herself that it had all been in her head. But it had seemed so real. Sadie had been so real.

Behind her, Dr. Benniton mumbled to himself. "Oh, Sadie. I would have given anything to see you once more."

As they passed the stairs that led up to the second floor, an icy draft dragged cold fingers across Mirabella's cheeks. She halted, shivering as much from excitement as cold. A gray mist formed at the top of the stairs. Mirabella watched as the figure grew more distinct. There, on the top landing hovered the outline of a woman.

Sadie.

The faltering clump and drag of Dr. Benniton's walker and footsteps stopped, and the house fell suddenly silent. Mirabella glanced back and saw him gazing up the stairs, a look of disbelief on his wrinkled face.

"Do you see her?" Mirabella asked, in a low whisper.

"No."

"But—"

"It can't be." The old man shook his head the way a swimmer does to shake off the excess water after getting out of the pool.

The figure came closer, floating down the stairs toward them, and the scent of roses filled the hall.

"Sadie?" Dr. Benniton let go of the metal walker and clutched at the wooden banister, pulling himself slowly up the stairs.

They met in the middle of the old staircase and stood face to face.

The apparition raised a hand and held it near the old man's cheek and he shivered. "Oh, Richard. I've missed you so much," she said, her voice a sigh of emotion.

"Sadie, my dear Sadie." He held out his hands to her and she placed her palms above his, holding them there, as if she were afraid to touch him.

Mirabella remembered how her hands had gone right through the ghost, how the only things she seemed to touch, she'd done so with her breath, or with a wave of cold air. How horrible, she thought, to love someone and not be able to hold them, or even touch them. She remembered her father the last time she'd seen him, how when she'd reached her hand inside the coffin, he'd felt cold and unreal.

Tears gushed from Mirabella's eyes and streamed down her cheeks as she watched Sadie shift and become more solid looking. Then Sadie's pale hands touched his and he pulled her into his arms. They held one another in a tight embrace, and he appeared younger, healthier, as if all the years and all the pain had melted away. Then something slipped and slumped to the floor and Mirabella gasped. Dr. Benniton and Sadie still stood on the stairs, holding one another and beaming, but Dr. Benniton's body sagged against the wall.

CHAPTER FORTY-EIGHT

"Dr. Benniton!" Mirabella screamed. She ran up the stairs and fell to her knees beside him. "Dr. Benniton?" She clutched his hands, but his limp fingers slid away like slippery ropes.

She grabbed his arms and called to him, but he wouldn't get up. She wanted to shake him, to pull him back, but he just lay there.

She knew she should do CPR or something! But she didn't know how. What if she only made things worse?

It was hard to breathe. She felt as if she'd been pushed off the edge of a high cliff, her breath coming in rapid spurts, her heart a stone that rattled and jumped against her ribs. Yards of tape seemed to be wrapped around her, covering her like a mummy. She laid her head on Dr. Benniton's chest and sobbed. "Please don't go," she pleaded. Her eyes were wet and she couldn't see. She thought she heard someone calling her, but she could hardly make out the whispery sound.

Sadie called again and Mirabella turned toward the sound

of her name. On the stairs above her, two figures embraced. Then the pale figures separated and turned toward her. Sadie pulsed and glowed. Beside her, the figure of a handsome young man stood tall and erect, Sadie's hand clasped in his.

"Dr. Benniton?" Mirabella's voice was a whisper.

"Yes," the young man said.

"But you're—"

He inspected himself, caught sight of the weathered body sagging against the wall, and his new form rippled like the surface of a pond when the wind whips across it. "So, it seems." There was a note of surprise in his voice. "But, oddly enough, I've never felt better." He gave Mirabella an apologetic look. "I'm terribly sorry I didn't believe you."

Mirabella stood transfixed by the two of them. Their outlines had begun to look smudgy and the glow that had been emanating from them since that first embrace glowed brighter, pulsing more and more in rhythm until they were in sync with one another. She recognized that pulse, it was the way Sadie used to begin blinking before she'd disappear.

"Please, don't go." She wiped the tears from her cheeks and rubbed her damp hands on her pant legs.

"It's time," Sadie told her. "My business with the living is finished. Thanks to you."

"And I'll be going, too," Dr. Benniton said.

Sadie sighed and her image fluttered out of sync with his. "No," she whispered. "You can't."

"I can't let you go, Sadie. I need to be with you." His spirit clung to hers.

"It isn't your time," Sadie's voice wavered and her image grew fuzzy. "You know I'm right. You can feel it."

"But—"

"You've spent far too much time in my shadow. It's time to let go. Time for you to finish *your* earthly business."

"No!"

"Yes," she whispered. "You must. You can't go with me. You can't move on till you're finished here. If you try to follow me now, you'll be trapped, just as I was. And we still won't be together."

Dr. Benniton turned to Sadie, her hand still gripped in his. "But I can't lose you, not again."

"I'm not leaving you by choice, my love." Sadie gazed at him with longing. "You know that. It's simply the way of things."

They embraced once more. Together their light shimmered as bright as the full moon on a clear fall night. The pulsing grew more and more rapid.

Mirabella watched in silence, tears cascading down her face. They turned and floated toward her, hand-in-hand, looking as if they were alive and walking down the aisle of a church on their wedding day. The light grew so bright Mirabella had to shield her eyes.

"Good-bye. And thank you." Sadie tilted her head to the side and blew a kiss at Mirabella. The cold air stung her tear-streaked cheeks, but there was tenderness in it, too. A sad softness that made her shiver, but turned her mouth up in a weak smile.

Sadie's spirit rose upward, growing smaller, as if it were flying high into the sky. Then the flashing figure disappeared, leaving the house smelling like a summer garden filled with blooming rose bushes. As Sadie disappeared, Dr. Benniton's spirit slipped down into his body, and the old man shuddered. A small wheeze escaped his lips.

Mirabella ran to the phone and dialed 9-1-1.

CHAPTER FORTY-NINE

Mirabella walked beside Dr. Benniton, holding his frail hand as the two Emergency Medical Technicians wheeled him out of the house. An oxygen mask covered his nose and mouth, and one of the EMTs held up a plastic bag that dripped fluid into a tube connected to the doctor's arm.

She had cried as she'd dialed 9-1-1, her voice breaking as the emergency operator asked her questions and told her to remain calm. The tears that wet her face were not only from relief that Dr. Benniton would be okay, but also from sorrow at losing Sadie.

There was also joy. Sadie and Dr. Benniton had found one another again, and although they had to part, they had both glowed so brightly when they'd been reunited, that shadows had danced in Mirabella's retinas when she'd dialed the phone.

One of the technicians nodded to Mirabella and Dr. Benniton squeezed her hand before letting go. The EMTs lifted him into the ambulance. One of them hopped into the back with Dr. Benniton. The driver swung the door shut, then climbed inside the cab of the vehicle.

Her mother's car pulled up, just as the ambulance revved to life. Her mother rushed up the walk as the ambulance driver turned on the flashing emergency lights and pulled out onto the street, siren blaring. She held out her arms to Mirabella. "Are you all right?" she asked.

Mirabella nodded her head, hesitated, then plunged into her mother's open arms and clung to her, sobs wracking her body. She'd thought she had finished crying, but fat salty tears pushed one another from her eyes, like school children running out to recess.

"Oh, Mira." Her mother squeezed her tight. "I'm so sorry. Did they say if he was going to be okay?"

Mirabella nodded and clung to her mother like a little kid, as if she wasn't in the fifth grade and already nearly as tall as her mom. Her mother was still warm from the heat inside the car and Mirabella shivered with the realization that she'd been standing out in the cold all this time without a jacket.

"Let's get you inside where it's warm," her mother said, guiding her back toward the house. Mirabella twisted away from her mother and hesitated, gazing after the retreating vehicle that carried Dr. Benniton away. She tried to get her jouncing heart under control. He would be okay. Sadie had said so. She'd said it wasn't his time, yet. Mirabella let out a shaky breath and allowed her mother to lead her inside.

In the kitchen, her mother wrapped her in a quilt and made hot chocolate for both of them. Mirabella sat near the stove, quivering under the heavy blanket in between sweet sips of liquid that sent warm tendrils through her. Her mother sat across the table from her, staring at her cup in silence.

She reached across the table to lay a hand on Mirabella's arm. "Are you sure you're okay?" She looked like she didn't believe Mirabella's nodded reassurance and gave her an it's-okay-you-can-tell-me-how-you-really-feel look.

Mirabella shrugged and took another drink of hot chocolate. How could she explain? She couldn't tell her mother what had really happened to Dr. Benniton on the stairs, couldn't tell her about the reunion between him and Sadie. She knew she could never mention Sadie to her at all, that it would have to be a secret between her and Dr. Benniton, because no one else would believe it. "I'm okay, Mom."

"I know how hard it can be to come so close to losing someone you care about," her mother said. "It's like nearly losing a part of yourself."

Mirabella snapped her head up. She had to know. "Is that how you felt when Daddy died?" She watched her mother's reaction as she said it. "Like a part of you went away, too?"

Her mother's eyes glistened and she blinked rapidly. "Your father . . ." Her voice cracked. She took a sip of her hot chocolate and started again. "Your father was in terrible pain. At least, in the moments that he was conscious."

"Is that why you wouldn't let me see him?" Mirabella swallowed hard and wiped at her eyes with the back of her hand.

"Oh, Mira." Her mother took a tissue and pushed the box toward her.

"I never got to say good-bye." It came out in a loud sob, louder than Mirabella had intended and she covered her face with a handful of tissues.

"Honey." Mirabella's mother got up from the chair and came around the table. She put an arm around Mirabella's shoulders and pulled her close. "His organs shut down and his body swelled with fluid. It was just so horrible and there was nothing the doctors could do for him." She was crying, now. Mirabella could hear it in her voice and feel the soft shudder of her body, as she hugged Mirabella tighter and rocked them both in a gentle motion.

"Your father loved you, Mira. More than the sun. More than the moon. More than the stars that he shared with you."

Tears poured from her mother's eyes and fell onto the quilt, making Mirabella cry even harder. She turned and wrapped her arms around her mother and squashed herself into her side. "I thought you hated him." Mirabella's voice was muffled, but her mother must have understood.

"Oh, no, Mira. I never hated him. Even when he decided he needed to leave us for a while and asked for the separation."

Mirabella raised her head and stared at her mother. "He decided? But I thought it was you who—"

"I know you did, Mira. But I also knew how much you loved your father, and I didn't want you angry with us both. I was waiting to see what he would do. Hoping, really, that he would come back to us." She pushed a curl of hair off Mirabella's forehead. "And then, after the accident . . ." She shrugged.

Mirabella began to cry again. "Mom, I'm so sorry." The quilt slipped from her shoulders as she stood up and buried her face on her mother's shoulder.

"I know, sweetie. I know. It's okay. Mothers and daughters don't always see eye-to-eye." She gently pulled herself away from Mirabella so she could look at her. "But as long as there's love, we'll always come back to one another in the end."

Mirabella thought about the love between Sadie and Dr. Benniton, thought about how it had taken years, but they had found each other again. It wasn't just mothers and daughters that could be brought back together by love. She smiled. Then she looked her mother in the eye and her smile dropped. "Mom," she said in a quiet voice. "You know I didn't have anything to do with the ex—that prank that Stacey blamed on me."

Her mother started to say something, but stopped. "I'm listening," she said.

CHAPTER FIFTY

The following Monday at the end of the school day, Mirabella stepped outside of homeroom to find Stacey waiting for her.

"Where have you been?" Stacey hissed. "You were supposed to meet me in the girl's bathroom an hour ago."

Mirabella licked her lips and opened her mouth to speak, but nothing came out. Her stomach tightened with queasiness.

"Give it." Stacey stuck out her hand.

Mirabella shook her head and tried again. This was hard enough without having to explain it. She hardly knew herself what had made her tell her mother about Stacey and Erin and doing their homework. They had stayed in the kitchen, talking late into the night, and Mirabella had found herself telling her mom all about it. The most amazing part was that her mom had listened and hadn't been mad. Disappointed, she'd told Mirabella, but not mad. And then she'd agreed to let Mirabella take care of it. To make things right. As long as she did it appropriately.

"Stacey," she began. "I'm sorry—"

Stacey narrowed her eyes and spoke through gritted teeth. "Either you give it to me now, or you'll be double sorry."

"No," Mirabella said. "I'm trying to tell you that I'm already sorry." She shifted her messenger bag higher up on her shoulder. "I'm sorry I ever let you bully me."

Erin walked up behind Stacey and listened to what Mirabella was saying. Her mouth opened and she shook her head in warning, but Mirabella ignored her.

"You can do whatever you want," Mirabella said. "It doesn't matter, because I've already told my mom everything."

"You what?" Stacey's face turned a darker shade of red.

"I talked to my mom. Last night." Mirabella looked past Stacey and her eyes locked on Erin's. "I told her how you both tricked me into telling you about my experiments. And how you've been blackmailing me to do your schoolwork." Mirabella kept her grip tightened around the strap of her bag. She was afraid if she let go, she'd be lost. "My mom knows everything, but she said she'd let me take care of it myself, unless I didn't want to."

Stacey glanced over her shoulder at Erin, then turned back to Mirabella with a sneer. "I don't believe you."

Mirabella pulled out the Hello Kitty folder.

Stacey's sneer turned to a triumphant grin. "Ha! I thought so. Nice try, though." She grabbed for the folder.

"Oh, this isn't for you." Mirabella held the folder out of Stacey's reach. "It's for the principal."

"The principal?" Stacey's mouth fell open. "What would he want with my homework?"

"It's not your homework," Mirabella shoved the folder back into her bag. "It's a confession. My confession about doing your homework for the past few weeks."

"I don't believe you." Stacey said, lunging forward and grabbing Mirabella's school bag. She jerked it off her shoulder and handed it behind her to Erin. "See what's in it," she ordered.

Erin took a step back and shook her head.

The weight of Mirabella's bag pulled Stacey's arm down toward the floor and she turned to see why Erin hadn't taken it from her, yet. "What's the matter with you?"

"I think we better not," Erin said in a quiet voice.

Stacey let her arm drop and the bottom of the bag thudded onto the floor. "What?"

"I just mean," Erin eyed Stacey through her bangs and swallowed hard. "I think we ought to just forget it." Her words squeaked out of her, like her throat was a rusty door hinge.

"You're in this, too." Stacey moved toward Erin, her voice menacing.

"Maybe, if we let her go, she might just let it drop?"

Erin appeared hopeful, but Mirabella was so startled by this turn of events that she didn't know what to say.

"Oh yeah. Sure she will. Just like I would." Stacey rolled her eyes and wobbled her head from side to side.

"She's not like you. She might just be nice about the whole thing."

"What's that supposed to mean?" Stacey said.

"I said, Mar—" Erin pursed her lips for a moment before continuing. "Mirabella," she said the name firmly, "isn't like you. She's actually nice."

"What?" Stacey shook with anger and Mirabella felt relieved that she was no longer the target of the girl's ire, but she also felt sorry for Erin. Mirabella knew just how much it took to stand up to someone like Stacey. She took a deep breath and stepped around her, snatching the messenger bag away from her at the same time. Then she spun around and stood shoulder to shoulder with Erin.

Erin huffed out a huge sigh of relief. "I guess this means we aren't friends anymore," she said to Stacey.

"Friends? Hah! Not likely. Like you were ever really my friend." She stepped toward the two girls, fists clenched.

"Good." Erin grabbed Mirabella by the sleeve and pulled her down the hall, around the corner, and into an empty classroom.

They sagged against the wall, waiting for Stacey to come barreling through the door after them. But she didn't.

"What just happened?" Mirabella finally asked.

"I think we just became friends." Erin did one of her cutesy waves.

"Really?" Mirabella tried to peek out into the hall without going too close to the door. "Do you mean like the enemy of my enemy is my friend, or do you mean real friends?"

"I'd like it to be real friends, if you're okay with that."

"I guess I am." Mirabella twisted her fingers together.

They were quiet for a little while. "Do you think she's out there waiting for us?" Mirabella asked.

"I doubt it," Erin said. "As long as the two of us stick together, she's not only outnumbered, she's outsmarted." She grinned at Mirabella. "Especially with you around."

Mirabella found herself smiling back. This might just be better than any experiment.

CHAPTER FIFTY-ONE

Dr. Benniton lay back against the white sheets, his head propped up on pillows. He was no longer pale. "I'll be out of here in a day or two," he said, his voice strong and sure.

Mirabella sat beside the hospital bed, examining the crisscross of tubes and wires connecting Dr. Benniton to the machines and equipment that surrounded him. A steady beeping sound marked the rhythm of his heartbeat. If not for her mother being a nurse and intervening on her behalf, Mirabella wouldn't have been allowed to visit him here. But because he had no living family or relatives, and because he had specifically asked to see her, the hospital staff had made an exception.

He leaned toward her. "To be honest," he whispered. "Since seeing Sadie again, I feel better than I have in years." He smiled, but his eyes glistened with unshed tears.

"I'm sorry she's gone," Mirabella said. Her throat seemed to hang onto the words, making her voice hoarse. She swallowed hard.

"I miss her, too." Dr. Benniton reached out and patted Mirabella's hand. "But I'm grateful to have had the opportunity to see her again. And I have you to thank for that."

On her first visit to see him in the hospital, Dr. Benniton had asked her to tell him everything, and Mirabella had told him the whole story. From the first chill breeze, to her argument with Sadie about the homework.

"She was always a stickler for honesty," he'd said. "But her students all loved her."

That had only been three days ago, just two days after his collapse, and already he was impatient to be released from the hospital. "There's a reason they say that doctors make the worst patients," he said, shaking his head. "It's because we're smart enough to know when our bodies are healed. Only, no one wants to listen to us. Bah." He let his head fall back onto the pillow and pushed the bed control so the head of the bed rose up to a higher angle.

"I almost forgot," he said. "I have something for you." He reached over and picked up an envelope off the bedside stand.

Mirabella took the envelope from him. Her name was scrawled on the front in spidery handwriting. He'd addressed it himself.

"I was going to wait, have Roger give it to you after . . ." He cleared his throat and turned his head away. "Anyway, I decided I'd rather give it to you now."

She scooted the visitor's chair closer to the bed before sliding her fingers under the flap and tearing it open. She pulled out the letter and unfolded it.

My Dear Mirabella,
From our talks, I know you have a bright

mind and it is my fervent wish to encourage you to reach your highest potential. Therefore, I have deposited funds in trust for the furtherance of your education. The enclosed paperwork contains the details of that trust. I hope you will see fit to turn your mind toward the study of science, but wherever your passion leads you, I believe you will succeed. It has been a pleasure to know you.

Your friend,

Dr. Richard Bilbock Benniton

PS: Thank you for helping to bring my Sadie back to me.

Mirabella looked up in surprise.

"I wanted to show my appreciation to you. For not giving up on a grumpy old man. For helping me to come to my senses in time . . ."

"But I can't take your money," she said. "I didn't do it for this." She held out the letter.

"Don't you think I know that?" He scowled at her, then his face softened. "Believe me, I don't give away my money frivolously," he said. "But I meant what I said in that note. You deserve this opportunity. And I want to be the one to give it to you."

Mirabella's cheeks grew warm and her scalp tingled with pleasure. She'd had no idea Dr. Benniton had felt that way about her. "Thank you." She leaned forward and took his bony hand in hers.

"All right, then. That's settled. I expect you'll do something wonderful, and I hope to be around long enough to see what it is."

"Thank you. I'll do my best." The pain of losing Sadie was still a fresh bruise on her heart, but she forced herself to smile up at him.

She hoped he'd be around even longer than that.

CHAPTER FIFTY-TWO

Mirabella stood before Sadie's grave, unable to lift her gaze from the two markers standing side-by-side in the fresh spring grass. Yellow marble, polished and carved, just as Dr. Benniton had described them. The one on the right had been etched with Dr. Benniton's name and birth date, an empty space where his death date would someday be carved. The writing on the one on the left had begun to show the signs of age and weather. The curving arches of stone bore etched roses that twined along the edges. Inscribed over Sadie's name were the words, "I love you," while the one that would one day be Dr. Benniton's marker read, "For sentimental reasons."

A swift breeze whipped her hair across her face, carrying the scent of the roses she held in her fist. She could almost see Sadie's spirit again, hear her telling them good-bye. The wind soughed through the trees like a satisfied sigh, as if the world had finally exhaled after holding its breath for a long time. Wherever she was, Mirabella knew that Sadie and Dr.

Benniton would be together again some day.

Mirabella's eyes got hot and prickly. She thought about her father. Would she ever see him again? She imagined Sadie asking her why she was crying. "It's just my allergies acting up," she said out loud, taking out a tissue and blowing her nose. "Dust and pollen." She dabbed at her eyes. "That's all." But she knew better. And so would Sadie.

At the edge of the green lawn, her mother waited, sitting on a polished wood and iron bench, her eyes closed and her face turned toward the sun. She seemed more relaxed than Mirabella had seen her in a long time. Mirabella wondered if it was because of the new house, or if it had more to do with all the time they'd been spending with Roger lately.

The new duplex wasn't nearly as big as the house on Rose Lane had been, but Mirabella had her own room and a backyard where she could lie in the grass and gaze up at the stars at night. Shortly after they moved into the new house, Roger had called to ask her mother out to dinner. Mirabella smiled, remembering how her mother had asked her opinion on whether or not she should go out with him, then how nervous she'd been after Mirabella told her she thought it was a great idea. Mirabella liked Roger. He'd always treated her like a person and he never talked down to her.

Mirabella was thinking about becoming a psychologist and, though she hadn't even started high school yet, Dr. Benniton had helped her research the best colleges for studying psychology. He knew a lot about psychology, and they'd had several excellent discussions about human behavior. He promised to take her and her mother to visit her top three university choices, as soon as she managed to pick them from the stack of shiny and colorful brochures sitting on her vanity. The same one that had graced her room in the old house. Aunt Clovinia had given her the vanity, telling her that anyone who appreciated a classic piece of furniture as much as Mirabella did should certainly own it.

She leaned down and placed the bouquet of yellow roses in the flower holder between the gravestones. Thick summer grass covered the ground in front of both markers. A few yellow dandelions still flowered among the short-trimmed spears of grass, but most of them had gone to seed, their white puffs bobbing on slender stems.

A warm breeze blew across the graves and the dandelions stirred and released their seeds. Mirabella sneezed and then smiled as the seeds danced in the air above the matching headstones, circling and bobbing around her, just as Sadie once had. The wind gusted, picking up the seeds and tossing them into the bright summer sky and wafting the scent of the roses to her.

"Goodbye," Mirabella whispered. "And thank you."

NOTES

While this book is a work of fiction, some of the topics are very real.

Polio

Poliomyelitis (polio) is a highly infectious disease caused by a virus that invades the nervous system. The virus lives in an infected person's throat and intestines. It is most often spread by contact with the stool of an infected person. You can also get it from droplets if an infected person sneezes or coughs. It can contaminate food and water if people do not wash their hands.

Most people have no symptoms. Symptoms, when they occur, may include fever, fatigue, nausea, headache, flu-like symptoms, stiff neck and back, and pain in the limbs. Less than 1% of infected people will become paralyzed, which may result in death. There is no treatment to reverse the paralysis of polio. However, many people recover some degree of muscle function.

Polio Vaccine

Developed in the 1950s, the polio vaccine used today has wiped out polio in the United States and most other countries.

There are two types of vaccine that protect against polio: inactivated polio vaccine (IPV) that is injected into the arm or leg and oral polio vaccine (OPV), which is taken by mouth. OPV has not been used in the United States since 2000, but is still used in many parts of the world.

Post-polio syndrome (PPS)

Some people who've had polio develop post-polio syndrome (PPS) years later. Symptoms include tiredness, new muscle weakness, and muscle and joint pain. There is no way to prevent or cure PPS.

Sources:

US Department of Health and Human Services: Centers for Disease Control and Prevention http://www.cdc.gov

The History of Vaccines: A Project of the Physicians of Philadelphia
http://www.historyofvaccines.org/content/timelines/po
lio

RECIPES

Mirabella's mom is a great cook. Here are a couple of yummy recipes from her personal files.

MIRABELLA'S FAVORITE EXTRA-CHEESY VEGETABLE LASAGNA

Ingredients

Two 15-ounce containers part-skim ricotta
2 large eggs
1/2 teaspoon kosher or sea salt
1/2 teaspoon cracked black pepper
2 cups shredded mozzarella cheese
1 cup shredded Italian cheese blend
1 cup Parmesan cheese
1 cup fresh basil leaves, torn
2 tablespoons olive oil
2 tablespoons minced garlic
1 yellow onion, diced
1 cup cauliflower, chopped
1 cup broccoli, chopped
1 yellow squash, diced
1 zucchini, diced
5-6 cups marinara/pasta sauce (homemade is best)
12 no-boil lasagna noodles (8 ounces)

Directions

Preheat oven to 400 degrees F.

In a medium bowl, beat or whisk together ricotta, eggs, salt and pepper. In a separate bowl, combine the mozzarella, Italian cheese blend, Parmesan and basil.

Heat a large skillet over medium-high heat and add the oil. When the oil is hot, add the garlic and onions and sauté for 1 minute. Add cauliflower and broccoli and cook for 1 minute. Add yellow squash and zucchini and cook until vegetables are tender (about 3 to 5 minutes). Season with salt and pepper. Remove from the heat and drain off excess liquid.

Spread one third of the pasta/marinara sauce in the bottom of a 9 x 13-inch baking dish. Place a layer of lasagna noodles on top. Spread a third of the ricotta mixture over the noodles, followed by a third of the cooked vegetables. Sprinkle with a third of the shredded cheese mixture. Repeat layers, ending with the shredded cheese mixture on top. Cover with aluminum foil and bake for 30 minutes. Remove foil and continue to bake until the top is golden brown (about 15 minutes). Let cool for 10 minutes before serving.

Makes 8-10 servings

Mrs. Polidoro's Savory Lentil Stew

Ingredients

2 tablespoons olive oil
1/2 cup chopped onion
1/2 cup chopped celery
1/2 cup chopped red or yellow peppers
1 tablespoon minced garlic
5 cups water
1 cup lentils, rinsed and sorted
1 cube vegetable or chicken bouillon
1/2 teaspoon dried thyme
1/2 teaspoon ground cinnamon
1/4 teaspoon ground pepper
1 large bay leaf
1 cup shredded carrots
Salt to taste

Directions

In a large saucepan, heat oil over medium heat. Add onion and celery and sauté until tender. Add chopped peppers and garlic; cook 2 minutes longer, stirring constantly. Add water, lentils, bouillon, thyme, cinnamon, pepper and bay leaf; bring to a boil. Reduce heat; cover and simmer for 20 minutes.

Add carrots; return to boil. Reduce heat and simmer until lentils are tender, stirring occasionally (about 20 minutes). Discard bay leaf. Add salt to taste.

Makes 4 servings.

ABOUT THE AUTHOR

SHARON SKINNER grew up in a small town in northern California where she spent most of her time reading books, making up plays, and choreographing her own musicals (when she wasn't busy climbing trees and playing baseball). She has been writing stories since fourth grade, filling page after page with fantastical creatures, aliens, monsters and, of course, heroes. She loves reading, drawing, arts and crafts, sewing, and costume-making (especially Steampunk). She lives in Arizona with her husband and four lovable cats. Her website is www.sharonskinner.com.

ABOUT THE ILLUSTRATOR

KEITH DECESARE has been a freelance illustrator for several RPG companies since 2001. His client list includes WotC, Kenzer Co. and Atlas Games. Born and raised in Arizona, Keith continues to hone his artistic skills ever since scribbling on a white wall with a black permanent marker. He uses a computer to do all his scribbling now with a leaning toward the fantasy/steampunk settings. You can check out his website at www.kadcreations.com

27199407R00127